UTAH'S BEST POETRY & PROSE 2022

SELECTED WINNERS OF THE
OLIVE WOOLLEY BURT
AWARDS FOR CREATIVE WRITING

CONTENTS

FOREWORD

LEAGUE OF UTAH WRITERS 2021
WRITER OF THE YEAR
CARYN LARRINAGA

Utah is famous for many things. Our powdery snow, our many state and national parks, our fry sauce—and our storytellers.

Whether or not every Utahn knows it, we are all spoiled by the number of poets, authors, journalists, essayists, and other wielders of the written word in our communities. These writers capture the weight of history, the emotions of the present moment, and visions for the future. They pass these moods along to readers worldwide and leave a lasting mark on everyone they touch.

In this first-annual collection, you'll find poems, stories, and personal essays which exemplify the immense amount of talent here in the Beehive State. Throughout the selection process, these powerful Olive Woolley Burt Award winners made me smile, cry, laugh, and most importantly, feel proud to be a member of Utah's writing community.

I hope you enjoy them as much as I did.

- Caryn Larrinaga

IN THE MARGINS

RUFO TOLENTINO

Trigger Warning: Suicide

SUNSHINE GETS UP from the bed. Perfume wafts through the air, a subtle scent with the hint of lilac. I appreciate her fake name. It feels like a sales tactic when a companion gives a legitimate-sounding one. Then again, I have no room to judge false pretenses.

I'm glad I found Sunshine. Her whole demeanor reminds me of Gema, not just her full figure, pale complexion, and blonde hair. When she walked in with fire-red lipstick and a dress pulled straight from a pin-up magazine, I knew she was the one. I've called on her ever since.

Sunshine blows a kiss before heading to the dresser. She takes the production of it all seriously, making efforts to not break the illusion.

I turn over, barely able to keep my eyes open. I shift my attention to memories, continuing my search for Gema. My hope is to find her in the margins, the moments between sleep and wake. I don't just *want* to find her there. I *need* to. Every night I fail to find her, our time together fades a little more.

Eventually, it'll shrivel into nothing. Like we were never together at all.

The sleeping pills start to kick in, keeping me from moving. But the awake self doesn't want to give in to the sleeping self. Not quite yet.

Since Gema has been gone, I haven't been able to fall asleep without assistance from medication. Consequently, it makes the window between sleep and wake shorter. I have less time to wander through the memories, trying to find one that sticks.

We're in front of a bridge. It's on a beach somewhere along the coast. I wrap my arms around her waist, pulling her close to me. The heat of her breath brushes against my cheek. A gust of wind blows her hair, and it gets caught in the stubble of my beard. I'm sure if I explored the moment further, I could recall details like time and place. But that's not what matters. The smell of ocean air mingles with that familiar aroma.

I miss Gema's scent. I sniff the air until I find a hint of lilac. It reminds me of her. That's why I ask Sunshine to wear the perfume. Gema's image materializes in the faded light of my closed eyes. I nestle deep into the memories, trying to evoke her arrival.

The opening of a dresser, the clanking sounds. Sunshine's care has made this not a routine but a ritual. She places Gema's things around the room. Little things. Hair ties, foundation, a little silver necklace—a ten-dollar sterling silver chain with a star pendant. A cheap little trinket that didn't mean anything. Until it did.

She didn't ask me if I'd buy it for her. There wasn't even a thank you. She just slipped it onto the counter of the bodega next to my bottled water.

Gema walks a few steps ahead of me. I don't know when we stopped walking side by side, but at some point in our relationship we got used to going at our own pace, letting the other person catch up when they're ready.

The ruffles of her poofy, black-and-white-checkered dress bounce up and down like a hula hoop. She walks too fast to successfully close her necklace. Her fingers fumble with the clasp, pushing aside her curly, blonde hair. Her gait slows, and I catch up. I tap her on the back with my free hand. Holding my bottled water with three fingers, I take hold of the necklace, trying to do the clasp while she continues walking. The bottle touches her back, and she cringes from the cold. She stops long enough for me to secure the necklace around her neck. She leans into me, and I close my eyes. All I have to do is open them, and I'll be able to see her face.

Something pulls me away from the memory.

Sunshine slips back into the dress she arrived in. She tries to be quiet about doing the zipper, which only accentuates the noise. Or maybe she's doing it on purpose, so I can hear the sound without waking completely.

The room in my mind transforms. The place that used to be *our* room but is now *my* room. I scan further and further back in the memories as if I'd pressed the rewind button on a remote control.

It's the first time I've laid on this bed. We were practically strangers, and it was still *her* room. My mind races as the water runs in the bathroom. What if she changes her mind? What if she doesn't come back? Was it presumptuous to undress? Heavy petting and rough kisses aside, it's our first date. What if she sees me here in just my underwear and asks what the hell I'm doing?

The water shuts off. The light from under the door disappears. The door opens, and my body tingles with anticipation.

A sliver of moonlight peeks in from the almost-fully-drawn curtain. As she walks closer, I only see parts of her body at a time. I see her thighs first as she saunters toward me. Then her hands, fingers playing with the tie of her silk robe. I can feel her weight on the bed and see her belly button surrounded by the folds of her robe and the lace of her underwear. The contours of her body peek through the light brown fabric, cleavage exposed as she slowly pulls the robe open. Next, her round chin, then her bottom lip, her bright red lipstick striking against her pale, white skin.

A few items jingle, then the zipper of a purse. The door opens and shuts, and reality floats further and further away.

I hear a giggle. It's distinctively hers. Not Sunshine's but Gema's. It's quiet in the middle but high pitched at both ends. She's on her way, and I'm floating to sleep. The scent of lilac lingers, connecting me to my beloved's memory.

I try to turn over, but I can't. The sleeping pills are strong enough to render me motionless. As I continue my futile attempts to move, the memories take on a dreamlike quality. I finally find myself where I've been trying to get for so many nights. Back to that moment where she and I could still be together. Half awake and half dreaming.

She's there. In the flesh. The first time in a long time. I've tried so hard to find her, and now she's here lying next to me. She turns as I turn, and we're face to face.

I remember every detail, every wrinkle in the iris of her blue-green eyes. Her hair is slightly more blonde in the summertime. Her dimples only come out when she's smiling or laughing. Her lips are asymmetrical, the left half of her top lip more puffy than the right.

The tears flow uncontrollably. I haven't allowed myself to feel anything for quite some time, my emotions muted by anti-depressants.

"What are you crying for?" she asks, wiping the tears from my face.

Her hand feels real. This moment feels real. I place my palm over her palm, never wanting her to let go. "It's been so long. I've missed you so much," I tell her.

She pulls my head to her chest. I wrap my arms around her, pulling her closer. Tighter.

After a few moments, she grabs my love handles. "You've gotten fat," she says. I hear that giggle again.

My hot breath bounces off her naked body as we break out in uncontrollable laughter.

I lift my head, looking at her. I brush the hair out of her face.

"I don't know how much time we have," I tell her.

"Why's that?" she replies.

"Because grief makes lucid dreaming way harder."

"Oh, I see," Gema replies. I forgot her dimples also come out when she's frowning.

"Let's go somewhere," I tell her. "We can go anywhere. It's a dream, after all."

"Sure," she says. "You want me to go like this?"

She looks at her naked body. She's lying on her side, one leg slightly above the other. Her breasts are pushed together, hidden by her arms.

"I can take care of that." I run to the dresser.

I see her things on top of the drawer, and the moment darkens like the lights in a movie theater after the previews, preparing for the main attraction. Seeing the pendant on the dresser, I wonder for just a moment if I've gotten up. I know, though, it's still a dream.

Now I remember why I ask Sunshine to place Gema's things on the dresser. Why the ritual is what it is. Why I've tried to recreate this moment so many times.

The sadness takes over, and the dream continues to break apart. One deep breath, then I reach into the second drawer. I take a pair of boxers and throw them on. Then, I reach in the top drawer for her silk robe. It feels heavy in my hands. Colors fade, and the light continues to dim as I grab the necklace from the dresser and walk back to the bed.

"Um," she says. "What is this? I thought we were going out?"

She sits up, slipping each arm into the robe and tying it around her waist. I sit next to her, fumbling with the clasp of the necklace.

"I just wanted . . ." I can't say the words. They're too hard, even now.

The world around us crumbles like plaster in an earthquake. No matter how long she's been dead, the dream will always fade into recollection. I can't stop the tears from flowing.

"I just wanted us to have a proper goodbye."

She's crying now too. "I'm sorry," she says. She kisses my forehead over and over. I can feel tears on her lips. She puts a hand on each of my cheeks, her face right next to mine. Almost the entire room has disappeared now. Only a few floorboards around the bed remain.

"I can't tell you why I did what I did," she says. "But I can tell you that I love you very, very much."

She can't tell me why because I don't know. I'm finally able to undo the clasp of the necklace, and I hold it out to her. She turns her back to me, and I place the necklace around her neck.

Everything goes dark. The room is gone. The bed is gone. Gema and I are the only construct I can keep intact. The only part of the dream that hasn't given into recollection.

I hear the tub overflowing in the other room, the memory overtaking my dreamscape. I don't want to be asleep anymore.

Because I know what's waiting for me behind the bathroom door.

I kiss Gema as she lays down on empty space, my hand behind her head. We kiss, her lips and tongue as soft as I remember. The water keeps running, and the dream fades. Her lips feel less and less real, replaced by the metallic taste of blood.

She's gone now.

It's just me, laying on my back, naked and cold. I'm half asleep and half awake, unable to move in the darkness.

I'm suddenly in the bathroom. Although this, too, is a dream, it feels like I'm really there. There's no running from this moment. I'm staring at it, watching it like a scene in a horror movie I can't turn off.

Gema runs the water, turning the stopper on the drain. She's getting a razor. She's undoing the ties of her silk robe and slipping into the tub. The water is turning red, and she's dying, and I can't do anything to stop it because it already happened. She's already gone.

I want out of this room, but there's no one to wake me. It's ironic that after all this time trying to relive moments with Gema, this is the one that brings her back. The one where I find her lifeless body in our bathtub.

I sit next to the tub, holding Gema's hand as the water runs red and overflows. The water rushes toward me, soaking my underwear. I think about turning off the water, but it's too much effort.

I don't know why I thought this would work. The moment in the margins doesn't last very long. Inevitably, the dreamworld takes over, and you lose control to whatever your subconscious clings to.

The rush of emotion after so much numbness is overwhelming. I was never going to be able to find Gema without reopening wounds. The memories I chose were always mundane, so nothing ever stuck. We shared fleeting moments in the margins. Images at the edge of the photograph. Did I know this was the moment I was searching for all along?

I thought I was obsessed with not getting a goodbye, but that's obviously not true. The love of my life died in a bathtub, wrists slit and eyes wide open. My real obsession was not knowing why. Because I thought we were happy.

My head touches the cold linoleum. Exhaustion takes over. I'm tired—of everything.

I blink, and the darkness returns. My eyes stay closed longer with each blink.

The darkness is all consuming. More than just my vision. Each time I shut my eyes, I'm more aware that both the dream world and the real world are just constructs. And each time I close my eyes, they cease to exist.

I can feel myself dying. It doesn't feel like a dream. It feels like sinking into quicksand, like falling deeper into the abyss.

I took too many pills. Was it on purpose, or do I want to run to the bathroom and puke them out? I couldn't get up if I wanted to.

Maybe I wanted this, to die dreaming of this moment, sitting next to her lifeless body, as if we're climaxing together one last time. Maybe that's our final goodbye. The one we deserve. A dark and broken goodbye. Two depressed people dying side by side.

Alone.

The hint of perfume returns. It's pulling me back from the abyss. Sensation returns to my body. The weight of my head presses against the pillow, my hands tucked underneath.

A rush of light and a blur of shapes and colors floods my eyes. I squint, the bright light telling me that it's now daytime.

The sleeping pills are still in my system. It takes considerable effort to sit up.

I rub my eyes, trying to shake off the medication hangover and adjust to the light of day. I'm not dead. It wasn't real. I let the dream world fool me.

The smell of lilacs prompts me to look at the other side of the bed. I knew Sunshine looked like Gema, but until now, I didn't realize how much. Her brown-blonde hair. Her fire-red lipstick contrasting her pale complexion. Her shapely figure.

She rustles in bed, and I see the necklace around her neck. I realize she's wearing the silk robe as well. It wasn't part of the arrangement, but it doesn't make me mad. I hear that giggle, the one that's soft in the middle and high at both ends. Then, I know.

"I'm really dying, aren't I?'

Gema rolls over and places her head in my lap.

"That's the thing about life in the margins, my love. You really can never tell what's real and what's not, can you?"

I stroke her hair, feeling the warmth of the rays of the morning sun and the heat of her flesh against mine. I know this isn't real. I'm not sure if it's heaven or just a dream. I'm not sure if I'll ever wake up, but I'm certain I'll hold on to this moment for as long as I can.

HOLIDAY

AMY LYNN HARDY

"THIS IS IT."

It's one of those phrases that echoes in your mind. So final, so definitive. *This is it.* The words sprawl across the room. It's in the way Mom says this time it was different when Dad fell —the way his eyes rolled back into his head was different— that crushes you like a slow-mo tsunami of truth.

"He's dying," she says.

And you know she's right.

But you're at Christmas Eve dinner with your boyfriend's family four thousand miles away with a glass of Merlot and a plate of *raclette* in front of you. Everyone's happy—in the holiday spirit.

This is it—it chokes you. You excuse yourself to go to the bathroom, hoping not to puke, thinking *shitshitshitshitshitshitshit*. A knock at the door ten minutes later reminds you they're all wondering.

"I have to go home," you explain. And your boyfriend is so kind and handsome standing there before you, and you wonder why you don't love him anymore. Maybe the trauma of cancer has carved too deep a canyon between you. Maybe you hate that he's so fucking normal when you're barely holding your pieces together.

One suitcase. Two doses of sleeping pills. Three flights. Four cities. Five films. Six time zones. Zero sleep. Infinite grief. Did you know that grief is an infinity symbol you wear, invisible, on your heart? At times, it's molasses slow, and at others, it accelerates like the loop-the-loop of a rollercoaster.

Dad's friend Ricky D. picks you and your boyfriend up at the airport in his truck. It's too late to visit Dad at the hospital, so Ricky drives you home. You try to sleep, but it's jagged and punctuated. You wake up every thirty minutes and wonder if this is really your life.

How could this be your life?

A trip to the hospital the next day lets you know it's the end and, like, *really* real, when the doctors say there's nothing more they can do. Slow-motion lips.

Nothing more we can do.

Five blinks later, a woman with microbladed eyebrows and crimson lipstick tells you about your "options." They're *all* hospice, of course—he's dying. That's the only option: keep him comfortable as he dies. So you watch your dad be wheeled into a van and shuttled to hospice, where he withers. Where you realize he will never see his home again. Where you realize he will never sit in his blue recliner again. Or make his famous ribs again. Or call you his "little bee" again. Petals falling from a dry rose.

He sleeps and sleeps, and when he awakens, he looks at you and says, "You're beautiful." He puckers his lips for a kiss when you leave at night. You have to feed him his last meals because he cannot do it himself. Nurses tell you he cries at night that he doesn't want to die. He regrets drinking and not listening to doctors' instructions. He wants to meet his future grandchildren and dance at your wedding. He wants to live—to *really* live. Your heart constricts like barbed wire.

The worst part is that you could have saved him. You had the chance to donate part of your liver. Doctors touched your abdomen and marveled at how soft your giant, healthy liver was. They told you that they rarely see women with such wide rib cages come in for testing. His sisters begged you to do it while your mother begged you not to. Tug-of-war. In the end, you kept your enormous, healthy liver.

You never tell him how much you love him because it's too horrible to fathom him not in your life. He's your dad. Your *dad*! Half of your DNA. Half of your roots. How will you live without him? Who even are you if he no longer *is*? You don't say goodbye, because you can't—it's too hard. This, you later regret.

You hear the phone ring on January 6th at 9:15 a.m. You already know who it is and what they're going to say, so you force your eyes shut and fantasize about screaming. Blessed, horrifying yelps.

"He's gone," Mom calls up the stairs, minutes later.

Your boyfriend rolls over and hugs you and tells you he's sorry and that he's there for you. But you know he won't *really* be there for you; there's an impossible distance between you now, a continental drift. You know he loves you in his way, but he doesn't understand. Not yet, at least. Somehow, it's not fair to let his untethered love seep like melting butter into the cracks of your barbed-wire heart.

You go through the motions. Death announcement. Phone calls. Flowers. A wake. The funeral. Drinks—lots of them. The vodka goes down so smooth, fills the emptiness. You tell people you're fine and then watch the slideshow your cousin's husband made for Dad's funeral and wonder if a person can die from crying. Against all odds, you wake up the next morning.

You fly four thousand miles back home and return to your normal. But it's not really normal. Is not knowing how to answer the question, "What do you want for dinner?" normal? Are brain fog and pulling the blankets over your head normal? Is wandering through your life in a stupor normal? Is pretending to be normal, normal?

You break up with that loving boyfriend. He knows it's the right thing too. Still, you both hold each other and cry.

You try to ignore grief, but it only makes you heavy and wretched. Like an unexpected assailant, it stabs you in your back when you least expect it. By summer, you have at least a thousand gaping wounds and wonder if anyone notices. Who sees the blood pouring out? The crusting scars? Anyone? You realize they see, but they don't know how to talk about it. Instead they offer platitudes.

"The first year is the hardest," they say.

"Losing a parent is a big one," they tell you.

"You're strong. You'll get through it," they reassure.

Christmas comes around again, and you realize it's been a year (a whole friggin' year!), and you've gained fifteen pounds and lost so much hair you could've sworn you were going bald. You've written a depressing novel and moved into your own place and seen on Facebook that your ex found someone new and prettier when you can't even fathom meeting anyone. BUT you're on the upswing; you know it! You can just feel it! Things are looking up. Plus, it's the holidays—the most wonderful fucking time of the year.

When you look closely, though, and scrutinize, Christmas stares at you with its eyes tilted to the side, like a broken-neck teddy bear that's been stuffed into the closet, watching through the cracks. "Remember how things used to be," it says. "Christmas is a joyous time, Amy. A blessed holiday."

Indeed.

(Happy) Holiday.

DRIVING WEST

JOYCE SCHMID

I'm riding shotgun in our old Renault,
three children in the back seat yelling
and the quiet one inside me.

The five-year-old leans out the window
singing, "Go-and-go-and-go."
The four-year-old complains, "I can't stop thinking!!"
as he sits and thinks.
The two-year-old's asleep.
The quiet one is turning
like a planet moving into day from night.

Years ago, I sang, "This Land Is Your Land"
to a hospital of veterans in wheelchairs,
though I only now find out what land is—

five hundred miles of farmland giving way
to Rocky Mountains slick with ice,
trees turned to stone,
the bones of dinosaurs *in situ* in the rock that buried them.

The car runs out of gas.
You hitchhike to the nearest pump.
I give the children apple juice and Barnum's Animals;
I read them fairy tales,
live-editing the ogres, and the giants, and the blood.
They listen, biting off the paws of tigers and the heads of lions,
as quiet, almost, as the quiet one.

We all survive the spells of Anasazi ghosts,
we all survive the desert made of salt,
we all survive the pass where people ate each other,
and we all survive the ghostly sight of San Francisco,
where at last we all arrive—

except the quiet one
who, uncomplaining, flows into the Bay,
and out to an undimmed sea.

THE LAST CHANCE

JOHNNY WORTHEN

RUTH WATCHED the car pull into the parking lot and knew, even before it had stopped, turned off its lights, and disgorged its single inhabitant into the flickering glow of the failing neon sign, that fate had crossed them again.

It was some kind of galactic weave, some strange unification of fates that kept touching her life to his. She'd noticed it before, commented on it, pondered it, even wrote about it in her diary, always with regret and a sense of failed destiny. It was coincidence, of course. The product of a small suburb and his rise to fame—a thing of perspective and confirmation bias —but still a nagging annoyance she couldn't help but fixate upon.

So it was that she wasn't at all surprised to see Pierce Malman step out of a rented car and, after straightening the lines of his tailored gray suit and running his fingers through his tousled, black hair, march to the door of the café and come in.

The Last Chance Cafe was a landmark and a dive. For half a century it had never closed, catering to early risers, lunch crowds, and the midnight denizens who needed food at 3:00 a.m. It smelled of coffee, bacon, syrup, eggs, and clandestine cigarettes. Hard-earned sweat. It had been made over several times, the most recent dating it by a decade with now-worn carpet and stained ceiling tiles. The lights always seemed brighter at night when the darkness outside was so thick. It stood as a beacon and harbor off Sixteenth Street, a pensive rest stop to refuel, recoup, and reassess. It was a pocket of slow time, especially so late as this, a place to catch up before moving on.

It was 3:05 a.m.

Ruth had worked at the café for four years and would see it to the end. The new Denny's by the freeway had finally nailed the Last Chance Cafe's coffin shut, and unless the café found a buyer within the month, it would be closed in two.

Pierce Malman—*Senator* Pierce Malman—blinked at the bright lights in the foyer and took in Ruth standing behind the counter next to the register. He saw and didn't see her. The waitress uniform was unremarkable; the lined face with little make-up was hard and nondescript. Thin and sinewy, so clothed and bedecked, she stood the very form of a func-tionary.

"A booth," he said.

Ruth took a single menu out of the box, wiped it with moist towel smelling of maple syrup, and, without asking if he was alone or meeting someone—a common question in the day but insulting at night—she showed him to the back of the cafe to a corner booth, where he spread out like an ooze and ordered coffee with four eggs over hard and toast without touching the menu.

"And a water," he said, finally making eye contact with Ruth.

His eyes were bloodshot-normal, the standard for customers at this time of night, and they showed no sign of recognition.

"Coming up," she said and went back to the kitchen.

Pierce took out his phone and scrolled through his messages. His mind fell back to Debby, his mistress, for just a brief moment, and he remembered leaving her on the bed in the apartment that he paid for, sleeping in a knot of red, satin sheets he required her to use. It was the briefest memory of drink, drugs, and sex. Rutting. Slaps. Sleep, then awake in the dark, needing to be gone.

Already congratulations had begun to flood in. His name had only been floated, not even announced, and already people were coming out of the woodwork to ride his coattails.

He looked up to see the waitress placing a glass of water on the table.

"You want me to leave the pitcher?" she asked.

"Where's the coffee?" he said.

"We're brewing a new pot. You wouldn't want to touch what we had, Senator."

"You recognize me." He smiled. "That speaks highly of my constituency."

"I know you," she said. "Do you remember me?"

He looked at her now, blinking against the fluorescent backlight. "Give me a hint."

"I'm Ruth Merriweather. I sat behind you in school."

"That's taking me back." He slipped into his patented capped smile, the one he used at work to get votes.

"You invited me to Senior Prom," she said.

"I don't think so. I went with Becky Sommors."

"You did. You asked me first and then canceled to go with Becky."

His smile slipped. "I don't recall."

"I went with Steve Caldeman," she said. "It worked out. I married him."

"I love stories like that."

"I was kind of mad at the time."

"Well . . ."

"I didn't like Becky so much either," she said, "so after all that, it was, you know, confusing."

"Coffee's up!" came a call from the kitchen, and Ruth left to fetch it.

He recalled the prom from "all that" so many years ago. Before the new movements. Before the new, politically correct inquisition of modern times. What he'd done was hardly out of the ordinary in those days, and it came down to a he-said-she-said situation that hadn't survived graduation. Becky had a reputation going in, and he was popular. It wasn't like he'd taken anything she hadn't already given away.

"Do I know that guy?" asked Carlos in the kitchen.

"That's Senator Malman," said Ruth.

"He's been in the news, right?"

"Short-listed for a Supreme Court seat."

"Shit."

"Yes," she said and took the coffee.

Becky had been the first time. Ruth hadn't seen it then, didn't understand what was happening. Had she done research then, she might've recognized the rising pattern, but she had her own life. As such, it became the first point on the map of coincidence that led to today.

Pierce considered leaving the café, getting the hell out of this shit-house town of an old suburb and back to Washington by an earlier flight. He'd left this town behind him after high school and only remained a citizen of it because its voting bloc was so secure. Once he got his seat—his lifetime appointment —he could finally flush this place, for good and all.

Ruth placed cream, sugar, and sweeteners next to the heavy, white, porcelain cup before filling it with fresh coffee.

"You've done quite well," she said. "The best of our class by far."

"I'm just here to serve."

"It was the Senchezi case that really skyrocketed you, wasn't it?"

"Everyone deserves a defense," he said, somewhat defensively.

"I was actually a reporter at that time," she said. "I was in the courtroom for much of it."

Again, he tried to see her as someone he knew. Thirty years ago, now twenty. "Did you wear your hair differently then?" he asked.

"I sure did." She giggled. "I was kind of a radical."

"Who were you a reporter for?"

"*The People's Standard.*"

He laughed. "Wow."

"Yeah, I know, right?" She laughed too. "Could hardly put that on my resume after the arrests."

"No." He drank his coffee black.

"They did get a little sensational," she said. "Probably had it coming after doxing the police force, but the Senchezi case, I thought, was handled well."

"Because you were writing it?"

She smiled warmly, her patented uncapped smile. The one she used at work to get tips. "Exactly."

There was a pause while they both remembered the case, and then she turned and went looking for his eggs.

Senchezi had killed three anti-police protestors and

wounded eight with his modified assault rifle on a cloudy April afternoon. The shooting had been live streamed by no fewer than eight witnesses, most from the "law and order" side. After a long time, the police finally approached and arrested him. The perp walk of him being taken to a police car, still with his rifle over his shoulder and eating a bag of Doritos given him by the deputy, made international news.

Defense attorney Pierce Malman had led his defense and got him acquitted. There were details and technicalities, charges of withholding evidence and tampering with some, plus a thick dose of blaming the victims. Senchezi walked. It had been a revelation to Pierce then. Before the verdict, he'd wondered about the world and his place in it. But after the verdict, all those existential questions were gone. The world was as the clever made it. Morality and justice were smoke-screens to be negotiated and ignored when opportunities arose. It was a dog-eat-dog world, and he was a big dog.

There were riots following the acquittal, and there was talk of a retrial, more police brutality, and more international outrage, but early snows put down the protests, and Senchezi died before Christmas. He blew himself up in his parents' basement while making a bomb. The blast killed six people: his parents, three neighbors, and himself.

For his part in the trial, Malman became famous in some circles, infamous in others. A self-proclaimed lightning rod. Unrepentant, unbowed. A guy who got things done. His fame carried him through to a House Seat, thanks to this secure district.

Ruth put the eggs on the table and refilled the coffee mug. "We crossed a third time," she said out of the blue, "when you broke ground for the Barger Development in what used to be the Three Creeks Wilderness District."

"That's a hell of a way to say it," he said. "Sounds like you're still working for *The People's Standard*."

"Oh, I've grown out of that," she said. "Reality is reality. Ideals like those are for the young and foolish, those who can afford to think past their next paycheck."

"Reality does tend to make people conservative."

"I remembered at the time watching you with that silver shovel, me and Steven and little Ted, our son."

"Wondering what?"

"Wondering how I kept running into you at these big moments."

"Prom?"

"And the trial, and the end of the wilderness, and the war."

"The war hadn't happened then."

"No," she said absently. "No, not yet. Teddy was so young then. But I remember looking at the wilderness, knowing it was a land grab for a mine and not the affordable housing it was sold as.

"Land is to use, girl," he said. "Barger found a better use for it."

"You know it's a Superfund site now, right?"

"Is it?"

"Yeah."

"Hmm."

"Enjoy your breakfast." She left him alone.

He'd made out pretty well with the Barger deal. A couple million in fact. It was how he became a Senator. The Wilderness had been nice, but the oil and lead pulled out of it had been far more economically impactful than the tourists looking for that endangered—no, now extinct—woodpecker. A lot of people got rich on that deal. None from that district of course, except himself.

"It's about being in the right place at the right time," he

said out loud to the empty table. Hearing his own voice, he looked around to see that he was alone. He laughed at his outburst, fatigue getting to him. "Timing," he said to wrap it up. "Success is about being bold, seeing the opportunities, and taking them."

"Is it?"

He jumped. Ruth was there with a dessert menu.

"I didn't see you come up."

"The cafe has a way of concealing things," she said. "These late hours are strange."

"Yeah."

"My son died in the war," she said.

"Which one?"

"Yours?"

"What?"

"Sorry," she said. "I've been on my feet all day. Let me get you a free piece of pie. What kind would you like?"

"Lemon."

She left, taking the menu with her.

It hadn't been his war. He'd only helped bring it about. How long could his country suffer the indignities of having their noble soldiers attacked for no other crime than that of having a base in the country?

It had been a quick war. He'd made eight figures in contributions and speaking fees, some he didn't even have to attend. The country had another puppet dictator in a strategic area. It had only cost a few hundred American lives. A few tens of thousands of theirs. Okay, maybe it was fair to call it his war. He'd been the flag-bearer for much of the debate. It made him a superstar with the party and got his name bantered around for the Big Job. Dogs eat dogs.

From across the café, Ruth watched Malman. He was the only customer. She and Carlos, the only employees. The morning staff would come in at 5:00. She calculated the minutes and again measured the times she had crossed paths with Pierce Malman.

While selling the war, he'd spoken at a rally in Arizona. It was surreal. She was there on her way back from Mexico, where she'd bought medicine that would slow Steve's death but not stop it. Ted was already in Basic, the only way forward to get to college and that architecture degree he wanted. Steve's cancer was incurable—had been from the first moment it'd been diagnosed since they couldn't afford the cure. Their insurance company denied the claim, and fighting it became as expensive as the treatment, leaving them bankrupt within a year. She recalled noticing, in the middle of all that, Malman on CSPAN as he filibustered the Insurance Commitment Act that would've saved her husband. But there in Arizona, on the tarmac, as Malman spoke, while she worried about customs finding the pills in her suitcase, she saw the coming war and found a new fear with her son's face on it.

Malman was an eloquent speaker. He could move audiences. And juries, she remembered. He could make the ridiculous sound plausible and rouse hidden depths of hatred and fear to the cause.

The people Senchezi had killed were black, Puerto Rican, and gay. The ones he wounded, liberals. He was white. How could he not have taken action in the face of such effrontery?

The war enemy was again brown, possessing worthless land between an oligarch's oil field and another oligarch's port. The papers didn't say that, of course. It was about patriotism and pride. The attack that instigated the cry was suspicious in a Gulf-of-Tonkin kind of way, but what of it? America, right or wrong, and Malman sold it. He could have been a preacher. He had a talent. Listening to him in the customs line, miraculously unsearched, she could only stare in awe at her old classmate.

The coincidences piled up in her mind then. There, in Arizona the pattern became clear, and for the first time it led her to an action. Not that she took it, but she saw it, saw the suggestion of what to do and colored it with the shades of missed opportunities and resulting events.

She couldn't, of course. Steve had needed her. She was a mother. She worked three jobs. She had responsibilities. She had too much to lose. And he was far away.

"Our children's children will thank us for what we do," he'd said that day at the airport. "It should not—cannot—be put off. If we do not act now, it will only be worse later."

Cheers from the crowd. She marveled at all the cleanly printed signs the crowd held up for him at this, his "unannounced" layover in Phoenix.

Steve died that year. Ted the year after. Three years after that, she had but one job and a hip that would need surgery within the year if she intended on using it in the next.

It was easy for her there in the bright cafe in the dark night to assemble the pieces of the puzzle, to connect the moments and the consequences, the certain realization of barriers and opportunities.

Synchronicity.

She limped a little as she carried the lemon pie to the table before collecting the dirty dishes.

Pierce cringed at her presence, waiting for more of her attitude, but she only smiled that smile, and he gave her his before sipping more coffee.

When she was gone, he leaned back and contemplated the pie, wondering why he was here. It wasn't like him to lurk these late hours. Insomnia wasn't his way. He concluded that the cocaine must have been laced with uppers and that he was excited about the coming nomination.

This would be better than the Big Job, which would be scrutinized and short-lived. He was getting tired of the scrutiny, the pageant, the pretend concern for people he despised. The Supreme Court, now there was a place to make a difference long term. There were hot cases coming up that made him salivate: abortion the perennial but also voting rights and property rights that would set precedent for decades if not centuries. He'd be able to weigh in on the Barger case, which was now at the Appellate Court. Best of all, he'd be the swing vote for the qualified immunity question. That was to say, he could remake the country in his own image. A smooth-running machine headed by the right people. The big dogs.

He was smart enough to understand this. Though his handlers from the party, from the administration, and even from the big guy himself talked in circles and analogies, he knew what was going on. There was a quick window now before the next congress was seated, where he could be put into place and secure the high court with little trouble.

The announcement was forthcoming; his midnight texts told him news was already out.

He decided to go back early to DC, be seen with the wife when the reporters came looking for him. He'd sleep on the plane.

"Bring me the bill," he called to the waitress, who nodded from the back of the café near the bus table, where she and some Mexican were talking, probably about him by the way they cast glances his way. Such it was to be famous.

He watched the waitress follow the man into the back and after a moment return and approach his table with the check.

"Is your friend there legal?" he asked her.

"I've never asked," she said, tearing off the ticket and placing it face down on the table.

"You should ask. It's your duty as a citizen," he said.

"My duty as a citizen?" She smiled broadly.

"What?"

Ruth produced Carlos's gun from her right front pocket, leveled it at Pierce Malman's forehead, and fired the single bullet that killed him at 3:46 a.m.

THE MAN WHO SINGS UNTIL...

RACHELLE KNAPP

Sleepy Mike Francis is lying in bed,
two fluffy pillows supporting his head.
His first love in life is not very far;
just a pillow away is his lovely guitar.

And just out his window, a moon and a star

Are watching and listening through sparkles and beams
and sneaking so quietly in all of his dreams

To make him so light to fly over the trees,
the rooftops and mountains, the dark silver seas,
with no fear of heights to wherever he please!

Hours pass as the moon travels the sky.
It knows all the while that the end is soon nigh.
But just before the sun takes its place,
it spreads its light softly on the curve of Mike's face.
For weeks will pass before it's back in this spot.

But the star and the moon, they haven't forgot

To shine and listen to his voice in the air,
surrounded by books as he sits in his chair,
singing so brightly with his soft, white moon hair.

His music will carry through the night afar
from this room of smiles and of songs
of three pillows
and guitar.

TORNADO

C. H. LINDSAY

Tornado hit my bedroom;
he wasn't very nice.
He knocked things off my dresser
and scattered all my dice.
Can't find the book I'm reading:
the one by Margaret Weis.
(I may just buy another—
it's not that great a price.)
He ran across my curtains,
then ate my doll of rice.
My bed is now a jumble.
My stockings have a slice.
He tore my favorite pillow,
a sachet full of spice.
My macrame's a tangle;
he climbed across it thrice.
He played with my computers
and tried to eat my mice,
then rolled across my keyboard . . .

the cord now needs a splice.
I often feed him catnip;
it was my friend's advice.
That's why my cat's Tornado.
My room: his paradise.

UNCOUPLETED

KEVIN LANE DEARINGER

I *suppose* that my heart has been broken,
Seduced by the lies you have spoken,
But I have heard them all uttered before,
And I find that such treacle is best to ignore.

I just *know* you regret this sad mishap
And your tender words doled out as scrap,
So I'm sorry I overreacted
To each promise you made. And retracted.

I've worked *hard* to face doom with decorum
And tried so to not blame it on boredom,
But all your lying has left me, you see,
Groaning alone with what must be ennui.

Will I recover and live? Time will tell.
But, lover, 'til then, I'll *see* you in hell.

MARMALADE REVERIE

AREN K. HATCH

A SEA of rubbish and junk surrounds me in the city's landfill. And then, right in front of me, I see it: an old watch with gold filigree and the initials of one R.M. Shroop. A vessel for part of a demigod's soul.

The broken and charming device fits perfectly between my thumb and index finger. I breathe on the face and rub the moisture away with the hem of my sleeve.

My regrets for losing the coin toss with Gideon melt away now that the prize is in hand. Our decades-long search, our years-long plan finally ends tonight. We get to see our life-long hero, the one who broke down the walls, who brought all the races together. Without Shroop's work, his beautiful, stirring words, who knew what Gideon's and my life would be like now. But I won't let myself think about it. Not today!

The journey out is treacherous, my soft-pointed, heeled boots leaping from one pile of dry trash to another between the foul and moldering organic material.

At the edge of the artificial fen, with one last leap, my heel slips on a rancid spot of grease. My body teeters every which way, and I fall on my back. Cold and sticky fluids soak into my hair and cover my hands; they even try to penetrate my heavy wool skirt and blouse. My palms squish into the old magazines and rotting fruit as I push myself up.

No leaping now. Instead, I slog.

When my shoes grind against stone, I break into a run, past the marsh hags screaming obscenities at me and hurtling odorous balls of muck. I scream with joy and thrill as they splat the world around me, but I'm too fast for any to hit. At the fence, I leap and catch my fingers on the wire. My toes wedge between the cracks, and, with the clock in my hand, I climb the metal and pivot up and over the top, letting myself fall onto the grass on the other side with a loud *oomf!*

The cries of marsh hags approach me, and a few balls of mud wedge in the fence. I tip my pretend hat to the landfill workers and break into a run again, passing through the magical barrier and trading the fen for tall, brick buildings with manicured gardens and fountains of ancient elven demigods. The landfill lies unseen and un-smelled behind the barrier, which projects the image of a lovely meadow.

Passersby pinch their noses as I sprint past carriages pulled by dracolisks and shopkeepers peddling new potions, fresh fish, and salted butterpops. I stop to snag a butterpop as the vendor looks away to some kids who probably mean mischief themselves.

I run again, watch clutched in one hand, butterpop in the other. Streetmen yell after me as I speed through the intersection and nearly cause a crash of carriages. One of them sends their dog after me, but the old mutt finds my butterpop more interesting than me. I toss it casually over my shoulder.

And then the busyness falls away as I turn into Caramelline Alley. I flip a coin to Old Sanny, the swamp nymph sitting behind her barrel and guarding the alleyway from ghouls.

"Three already today, Tetra!" she cries as she catches my coin with a gelatinous hand. She places it between her teeth and chitters like a raccoon. "As delicious as ever!"

"Only the best for you, Sanny!" I tip my invisible hat again and turn the corner into the dead end, coming to a stop by the brick wall.

I rap my knuckles on it. "Delivery!"

Gears grind, and the heavy tumbler spins as the door unlocks and the brick wall shimmers. With my toe, I open the hidden door wider and pass through the illusion into a dim-lit, figure-eight-shaped room with a matching mezzanine above. Slipping off my soiled boots, I set them next to Gideon's pristine, mahogany suede pair.

"No butterpop today?" I hear from overhead, followed by a deep sigh.

"I think I've found a new use for them." I walk into the lift in the center of the room and extend the watch up toward the hole. Gideon snatches it from me. With both hands free now, I pull on the rope to bring the lift up to the mezzanine.

Gideon, my dryad partner in crime and magic, sits cross-legged, face covered with an auramask as he inspects the clock closely. "Don't think I can't smell you, either."

"I need new shoes. The trash almost took me! Can you imagine? Me as a marsh hag?"

"Yes, indeed. You're already halfway there."

I stick my tongue out and wander away as he says, "Oh yes, quite mature of you."

"Quite." I step up to the bottom of the spiral staircase that leads up the tower. "How's the view?"

"It'll be splendid viewing tonight. And oh so quiet."

"You don't want to be in the streets with hundreds of noisy people and screaming children?"

"I'll take the marsh hags." He lifts the heavy welder-like

mask to the top of his head and fixes me with keen seafoam green eyes above a—

Human nose!

I slap a hand over my mouth. "You didn't."

With a derisive sniff, he says, "Please, if you could withhold further judgment. My bones already ache with an embarrassment impossible to define in such petty linguistic terms."

"Oh, but *why?*" I ask. "Not for Shroop, surely? Your continent and ours didn't know each other back then, but Shroop advocated for unification of all races. They won't judge you for not looking like a human! Your barkskin is lovely."

Gideon harrumphs and snaps the mask back down before standing and hopping down to the ground floor.

Hands on the railing, I watch him strut to his lab in one of the rounded corners of the figure eight. "Oh, Giddy. You'll ruin your eyesight with that mask. You'll see auras in your sleep. And the doctor will be upset if he hears you've given yourself nightplagues again."

After a sullen pause, Gideon pulls the mask off. "I can't look like this tonight, not in front of Shroop. How am I supposed to tell them how much they mean, not just to me but to all non-human races, while looking so ridiculous!"

"I'll find some cherry bark liniment," I say, "but you know how your body reacts to it. It'll cause such a mess. Or you could pretend it doesn't bother you, and they won't know the difference. For all they know, dryads have human noses with human skin even though the rest of you is barkskin." I giggle over my knuckles. "It's a bit adorable, actually."

"What was I thinking, Tralala?"

"It was the jitters. Too *giddy*." I laugh and take the lift down to join him at the worktable. "How can I help?"

"Bathe and then fetch me a butterpop while you're out

looking for liniment. When you're ready, we can pull Shroops's soul shard from the watch."

Phony magic, the university called it. It would never work, they said. After decades of independent study, we'll show them tonight.

I bathe in Gideon's deep copper tub and pull on fresh clothes, though the filthy boots are all I have to wear.

In town, the shopkeeper is happy to sell me two butterpops and a sack of scotch chews, none the wiser about my earlier pilfering. The cherry bark liniment takes most of my coin, but it's worth it.

People are already lining the streets, and children run over the cobblestones collecting trash to send the marsh hags' way.

In the alley, I toss another coin to Sanny, who says, "You better get in there. I heard a noise."

I enter without announcing and walk into a thick cloud of salmon smoke. Juggling my buys in one hand, I wrap my scarf around my mouth and nose. The smoke swallows my words when I try to speak, spitting them back out as a cough. So I stumble in the direction of the workstation and bump into something soft. No, someone, and—

"Oh my," I say.

A tall elf stares down at me with beautiful big eyes, the same salmon pink as the smoke. They wear an outfit of shiny, crisp fabric, the stitches glowing like fireflies. A magic find-me! thread sticks out of a breast pocket—at least, if my memory serves me right. A vivid orange cape rests on their shoulders, and coarse blond hair gathers into a mess on top of their head.

They point at me, the fabric of their jumpsuit crunching. "Is that your name?" they ask. "'Oh my'?"

"Tetra!" Gideon bumps into me, the flowers on his crown frazzled and the new human nose red with irritation. I gesture to the smoke, and he vanishes. A moment later, a gentle wind caresses my face as the smoke whisks out the window, directed by Gideon.

"You!" he shouts, gaping at our guest.

The elf nods. "Yes, me."

"R-r-r-r—" Gideon tries.

I take charge and extend a pop. "R.M. Shroop?"

"Delightful." They take the pop and bite off a chunk.

"One moment, Mx. Shroop." Taking Gideon's arm, I pull him aside. In a hushed voice, I ask, "What in all exuberance happened?"

"Well, I *might* have started tinkering with the watch already, and I guess their soul shard was eager to escape." He peeks around me at the elven demigod and grips my wrist. "Suns and moons, Tralala, they're actually here. They're real."

The light drains from his eyes. "And they're seeing me in such a dismal state." He moans and turns away, clutching both sides of his head.

"Oh, Giddy, it really makes no difference to them! They've never even seen a dryad before."

"A what now, you say?"

Gideon freezes, and I turn around, offering my best winning smile. "Forestfolk from a different continent." Before I can stop myself, I add with a nervous chuckle, "Dryad's don't have noses like us. He just wanted to emulate you because he admires you so much."

Beside me, Gideon offers the most pitiful whimper.

Shroop's face contorts in both thought and confusion, their finger absentmindedly reaching up to run along the slope of their own nose. "An entirely new continent. My, my. But if he were such a creature, what would he be doing here in these walls of stone?"

"The books are forest enough, aren't they?" I say.

Shroop's face twists into a smile. "And why have a *dryad* and a fairy brought me back to this wretched world?"

"I know you lived during a time of war and famine, Opulence, but it's all different now. Peaceful. Joyous."

"Leastwise, for the time being," Gideon says.

I elbow him and say, "They're holding a parade tonight in your honor."

"My honor?" Shroop echoes, like they can't fathom the sounds of it. They stick the butterpop in their mouth and slowly pull it out, a thinking glimmer in their eye. When it exits their mouth with a fitting *pop!* they say, "I seem to recall throwing my watch into the Wildershire Wastes."

"It was found eighty-seven years ago," Gideon says. "When Tetra and I were but tweens. Mr. Polliver kept it in his house all these years until—"

"Long story short," I say, "we stole it from him. His security doesn't check the waste before it's sent to the hags."

Gideon says, "Mr. Polliver keeps sending ghouls to sneak in and catch us in the middle of something, but we have a refined security system."

Shroop paces the room, butterpop securely in hand. They cut a striking figure among the books and ancient wood. With each turn, they flourish their cape, pause, and continue forward.

"No need to emulate me," they say. "One should take pride in one's natural features."

Gideon throws his hands over his nose.

Pulling the bottle from the hidden pockets of my skirt, I say, "I bought some liniment to break the spell, but barkskin doesn't much like it. Have to stay six feet back if you don't want to get thrown into a wall."

Shroop hums to themself, and their gaze finds the spiral staircase. They stick the pop in their mouth and throw themself up onto the mezzanine. They arrive at the base of the stair-case before Gideon and I have time to process.

By the time we make it to the mezzanine, Shroop is up the stairs and gone.

We ascend the steps and onto what Gideon has fondly named the Battlements. The two of us split, bend over the railing looking for Shroop's marmalade cape, and meet back at the stairs.

"Oh dear. We've lost our demigod," Gideon says. "If Polliver and his ghouls find them, Shroop's as good as gone. Polliver will find some way to capture them, I'm sure of it. To spend one's final day in the clutches of that horrible man . . ."

"Then let's chase them!" I grip Gideon's arms. "Do not lose your bravery now, Giddy. This is the day we've dreamt of for decades. Think of everything you want to say to Shroop! You can't let a little thing like a nose keep you from it!"

Gideon shakes his head and covers his face again. Muffled, he says, "Please, you can't make me."

"Gideon Grawn, you look at me, and tell me the last time you cared so much for the opinions of others! Not when you paraded through town in your chicken suit because you'd forgotten the play that night, so wrapped up in helping Eloise with her birthday party. Not when the librarian dropped a bucket of mud on you for being too loud in the library the day you learnt of diamond griffons!" I stomp my feet. "I can't recall a time! What would our demigod say to such cowardice?"

"Perhaps my emulation was so offensive they left!"

"Giddy," I laugh. "Remember all the reasons we so adore Mx. Shroop! The little things."

He looks off to the side as he recollects the thousands of words each of us have read on the demigod. "They . . . hated walls. Were always caught sneaking out of meetings to run free in the . . ." Gideon brightens, and buds sprout from his skin. "In the streets to play with the children and race with their dogs."

"Buying orange jelly rolls for everyone before the others found their find-me! thread and dragged them back," I finish. "What are we going to do, then?"

Gideon lowers his hands. "Drag them back before Polliver ruins it all."

The two of us rush down the stairs. Gideon puts his patchwork cap on just off-center, and in the alley, the two of us offer coins to Old Sanny.

Our feet touch the threshold when her croaky voice wraps around our waists and twirls us back to her.

"Please, Sanny, we've a mission!" Gideon says.

Sanny wags her finger and pushes herself up onto the barrel. "Well, then I'm not of a mind to tell you what Caramelline Alley's just seen."

"A demigod with a beautiful, orange cape?" I ask.

"No, a handsome human with a dangerous glint in his red eyes," she says. "Came to see what's kept his ghouls at bay so long, I expect."

Gideon falls back into the brick wall. "Oh, we've already lost them to Polliver. He'll have seen. He saw, didn't he?"

"The funny elf with the pop? It's dangerous to jump from roofs with food in your mouth." Sanny grunts and slides back down to the ground. "You best be following after them. Mr. Polliver's not as quick as that stranger, but he's keener than anyone I've ever seen."

I toss another coin to Sanny, and she bites down on it with glee.

"Come sit with us tonight, Sanny. Best view in the city, and all the apricot sandwiches you could want."

I take Gideon's hand, shout, "Come now, Giddy!" and pull

him into the street, where we narrowly miss a collision with a carriage. Gideon cries out, the driver curses, and I laugh. We maneuver around carriages and wagons to the angry calls of more drivers and hisses of dracolisks.

Beside me, breathless and holding his hat to his head, Gideon says, "Do you even know where you're going, Tetra?"

"Of course!" I've no idea. Like Shroop often described for themselves, I let my feet take me.

The smell of the street, the sounds of its people, and everything's energy here smolder red like Polliver's eyes, grumpy and rigid. As we turn into another street, away from the parade and its demands, the red shifts to a pleasant violet. It's all in my head, of course, but Shroop would admire the effort. My fairy imagination.

Gideon tugs on me to stop, and we skid beside a fruit cart. He doubles over, bark shuddering with every labored breath. The vendor blinks and offers him a bowl of ice water and nectarines. Gideon straightens at once and dumps it on his body. It soaks into his skin, and the sprouts and branches wriggle in joy.

A golden vibe tickles my ear. I wander toward the end of the street and rest my hands on the colorful, stone barrier overlooking the beach. Boats float tied and empty at the dock, a sleepy dockmaster on his stool watching over them.

The energy emanates from him.

I find the stairs and race down.

Up above, Gideon calls my name, but I leap onto the sand. My heels dig in deep, so I unbuckle them and prance to the wooden docks.

"Tetra, what in all exuberance?"

The energy centers around the dockmaster but not from him himself. The old codger continues snoring as I stand beside him. In his breast pocket lies Shroop's find-me! thread, the beginning of old elven hide and seek.

I pull it out and back away, knocking right into Gideon. He lets out an *oof!* and falls. "I'll have sand in my knots for days now!" he grumbles as he stands and pats himself off.

He peeks around me. "What's this, then? No, it can't be! Is it really a find-me! thread?"

I offer a mischievous smile.

"Maybe you were right, Tralala, as you so often are." He flashes a bashful grin, before looking away to hide the sprouts of embarrassment springing from his cheeks and around his ears.

"May I?" he asks and pinches the thread.

On the count of three, we tug on each end. The thread swirls into the air and splits into a dozen tiny fibers that knit into orange flowers. The breeze takes them over our heads, a petal falling to the ground as the others soar to the north.

My shoes fall from my fingers as Gideon and I race after the flowers, which pirouette in the sky like a pair of lovesick birds. We make sure to always keep an eye on each other or on the flowers that no one else can see. Holding hands, we side-step around horses, people, and streetlamps.

The petals lead us to the main square. The crowds separate Gideon and me, but we dart between folks, our eyes catching one another in the space between crooked elbows or the showers of tissue paper children spread by the fistful.

The last flower flies over the fountain.

We step onto the rim on opposite sides and walk along the marble toward each other. As we meet, he offers me a hand down to the ground.

The flower drops a petal onto our heads.

We meander through the crowds to the edge of the plaza and a small lane.

Another petal falls.

As I reach for Gideon's hand, the crowd swallows him up.

"Gideon!"

I can't leave him behind, but neither can I lose the trail. Turning, I smack into a tall man with a long, black cloak, velvet waistcoat, strong chin, and— "Oh."

Mr. Polliver's deep red eyes are filled with reproach. "A pleasure to meet you again, Tetra Teakander."

Gideon's warmth manifests at my side.

"And you, Dr. Gideon Grawn. Or no . . ." Mr. Polliver smiles. "You've been stripped of that title, haven't you? What a loss that must have been for the dryad who was once the pride of his university."

"I lost the title, not the achievement, Mr. Polliver," Gideon says. "In the end, its loss takes away none of the things I have gained."

"But we realize that must be hard for someone like you to understand," I say with my heart in my throat. "Seeing as you don't have any real accomplishments of your own. Fruits of a greater sire, are they not?"

Mr. Polliver's smile twists into a sneer, and he lifts his hand. Four large men emerge from the shadows, taking Gideon and me by the shoulders.

"You have no right to do this," I say, watching the flower float down the lane and out of sight.

"You may speak to me of rights when you prove you did not engage in criminal theft during my auction." Mr. Polliver leads us into a small alley. Two ghouls stand at the other end, their tiny, hunched bodies almost invisible until they turn their chartreuse eyes on us.

The goons push us against the wall, and Polliver pulls out a pair of mulberry velvet gloves.

Gideon squeezes my hand.

As he puts on a glove, Polliver says, "You will confess to me your crime and also locate that peculiar elf."

"What elf?" Gideon asks, his voice an octave higher.

Polliver starts on the other glove. "You fooled me enough at the auction, Grawn, perhaps because Teakander did most of the speaking. But you cannot fool me now. You unlocked a shard of Shroop's soul from the watch, and mark my words, you'll tell me how, or you'll see a prison cell in the Dark Sea among the salt hags and venomous snails. For now, I'll be satisfied with finding Shroop's shard. It doesn't have long, does it?"

He bends over to look me in the eye. "Find them, Archmage Teakander, or I will introduce you to friends who can tear a fairy's magic from them."

"That's not possible," I say, thankful the shaking keeps out of my voice.

"Ah, but you've heard the rumors. And they would love to get their hands on an archmage who forsook her power to help a washed-up mago-historian."

"I didn't leave the order for Gideon," I say, adding quickly, "Sorry, Giddy."

"This is your last chance," Polliver says. "Find me Shroop, or pay the bitter consequences."

A plan enters my mind. I release Gideon's hand and step forward. "You make a convincing argument. I'll take you to them."

"You will?" Gideon whispers.

"I'll not see you harmed, Giddy. Trust me." I wiggle my nose and lightly pat my pocket, which is hidden by the folds of my skirt.

The goons push us into the lane.

We'll be okay. Thank God for Gideon and his horrible but strangely cute human nose.

"Walk on, then," Polliver says.

I lift my chin and walk down the lane, turning left where the flower did. A disintegrating orange petal on the cobblestone reflects the setting sunlight. My hands clasp behind my back, and my feet half skip over the stone.

Polliver mutters something about the foolishness of fairies.

The last petal lies on the base of a streetlamp. Beside it, a staircase leads down to the park. I extend an arm. "After you, Mr. Polliver."

He narrows his eyes and gestures for a couple henchmen to go first. As we head down, children's laughter reaches our ears. The steps end at a gravel path that winds its way around shrubs and little trees to the river. A marmalade cape drapes down by the rushing water's edge, flanked by six children.

Mr. Polliver struts over to Shroop. "Pardon me, Opulence."

Shroop and the kids look over their shoulders, and the demigod gives Polliver an unimpressed up-down. Then, their sight lands on Gideon and me, and I wave. They smile and lift that charming smile to Polliver.

Polliver clears his throat. "Greetings and salutations. I am Mr. Armand Polliver, owner of—"

"Now, observe, children." Shroop stands. "The wealthy man, this one particularly devoid of compassion and the ever-sought-after empathy, stands before us, I think, to engage in conversation. To what end, one has to wonder."

Polliver scowls. "What?"

Shroop and the children circle Polliver. "He takes offense! Perhaps that is why he brought backup, because he lacks the strength and wit to fight his own battles. Indeed, I know the very type, as I oft battled with his kind. Albeit in none so pleasant a place as this. And look! He even brought prisoners. Perhaps to extort us."

"I do not wish to play games," Polliver says and curls his hands into fists. "The fact is, you're my property."

"An individual? Property?"

"You know very well you're nothing more than a shard of a once-real individual," Polliver says. "Shards don't have rights. You will come with me peacefully. I'd rather not do anything rash in front of children."

I reach into my pocket and pull out the liniment. Shroop's eyes glance at me as I do. Do they remember what happened what I said? Six feet back?

Their smile turns dangerous. "You *do* like your threats. And yet you do not see the real threat!"

"Oh?" Polliver asks with barely contained rage, his body shaking. "And what is that?"

Shroop points at Gideon. "A dryad with a *human nose!*"

As Polliver turns, Shroop twirls their cape around the children, and I pour liniment on my hands. "Sorry, Giddy!" I slather it on Gideon's nose, push him toward Polliver and his goons, and fall flat to the ground.

"What is the meaning of—"

Full branches and leaves shoot from Gideon's body, smacking the goons in the gut and pushing them right into the river. Gideon lurches toward Polliver, who tries to flee too late. A tangle of flowers wrap themselves around his legs. Polliver reaches for a nearby tree, but his gloves snag. Slipping out of the velvet, he tumbles into the river with his goons.

The children clap their hands and jeer as the crystalline water shoots the men away, toward the city's edge.

Gideon retracts the branches and flowers, giving one last great sneeze before his human nose flattens and turns back to bark. His whole body shudders. "Let's not do that again," he says, voice stuffy as if with a cold. "*I* won't do it again."

"I see you found me, then," Shroop says. "I was hoping you would, though I did not expect quite a show!"

"Neither did we." I wrap an arm over Gideon. "Will you watch the parade with us?"

Shroop holds up a finger and crouches down, ruffling the hair of one of the children. "My newfound friends, I must leave you now. But!" They pull a tiny bouquet of flowers from nowhere, with one flower for each child. "Remember the things you have learned today, and I promise you will live a life full of absolute wonder."

By the time we make it back to the Battlements—Sanny on Gideon's shoulders—the parade has started. The sun dips near the horizon, but from where we sit, our feet swinging over the ledge and apricot sandwiches in our sticky fingers, the whole town lights up the festivities for us.

Shroop sits between Gideon and me. Occasionally, Gideon and I swap looks behind their back as if to ask, "Is this finally it? It's happening? Are we sitting with *R.M. Shroop*?"

Warmth fills my heart, the kind I haven't felt since Gideon presented to the Archmage Order on something entirely lost to me now. Here we are, still together, our dream realized. It was so long in the making only to last a day. But it was worth it because all the naysayers who said we'd never find the watch or the right magic to open it were wrong. It took us nearly our whole lives, but we did it.

I'm happy. And I know Gideon is too. I see it in his seafoam eyes and in the little flowers that bloom all over his skin in every shade of yellow.

As the parade approaches our street, Shroop says, "I do believe this is the most perfect way to spend my last hours in this curious world."

Gideon says, "You don't mean to say that was the only shard?"

With a tender smile, Shroop says, "I made but one. Anything more seemed too greedy. Even now, sitting here watching this . . ."

"I'm the greedy one," Gideon says. "I've wanted this moment my whole life. I know it might seem crazy or creepy. You wrote the draft for the treaty that eventually brought us all together. I know you didn't get to see it in your lifetime, but now you can. You can see how thankful we all are."

Shroop closes their eyes. "You're very kind to say so."

"It's the truth," I say. "You brought Gideon and I together. You brought everyone together."

"It's . . . such a relief to hear, to see. Thank you." They laugh and open their eyes. "My apologies for running away earlier. I had to. Just one last time."

I wouldn't have had it any other way, and I know Gideon wouldn't either.

"Say," Shroop says. "May I ask one last thing?"

"Name it!" Gideon says.

Shroop watches the street with sparkling eyes. "I desire another of those excellent candies."

"Candies?"

I lift a knuckle to my lips. "Butterpop. Of course."

Gideon sighs happily as he eyes the floats and dancers. "We'll get you all the butterpops."

I take Gideon's hand behind Shroop's back, our fingers interlocking. As I join in on the parade-watching, I say, "Every single one."

QUENCHED

SEPTEMBER ROBERTS

TWENTY YEARS. That's how long Veronica had waited for him.

She pulled her phone out of her back pocket for what must've been the hundredth time. Still nothing.

What did she expect? That he would call? Did he even know her number? After so long, would he even remember their pact? It was all she could think about, but that didn't mean he did.

"Anything?" Stephanie asked.

Veronica shook her head. "I'll give him until midnight." She sighed and checked the clock. "It's ridiculous. I know."

"It's romantic, not ridiculous." Steph hip checked her and smiled. "Maybe you should cancel your class and go find him. I still can't understand why you wanted to teach on your birthday. You should be out there, sweeping him off his feet. That would be swoony."

"No. When we broke up, he said he would come find me in twenty years. On my birthday. That's what he promised."

Veronica fingered the pendant hanging around her neck as she always did when she thought of him, which was often. A few days ago, she'd doodled on her hand while waiting for customers, connecting the freckles, starting to spell his name. The faint G of ink still showed at the base of her thumb. Six years ago, she had made a pendant matching that G and hadn't taken it off.

Two women came into the shop. "We're here for the ring making class."

"You're in the right place," Veronica said with a smile, pushing all thoughts of *him* out of her head. "Why don't you head back into the classroom and get situated. We'll begin in a few minutes." She pointed to the corner where all the supplies were set out.

"Um, V? Can you come up here, please?" Steph called from the register.

With a handful of sterling silver wires in her hand, Veronica made her way out of the classroom. Her breath hitched as she took in the sight of the tall man chatting with Stephanie. There's no way those broad shoulders could belong to anyone else. Gabe had remembered.

———

A soft, metal tinkling sound drew Gabe's attention. Veronica stood there, a delicious pink flush spread across her chest and neck. She looked even better than he remembered. He took a second to take her in, from the full curve of her hips to the bit of freckled skin exposed below her collarbone. How many times had he kissed along that delicate skin? Why had he taken her for granted? How long had he been staring at her? Embarrassment heated his cheeks as he picked up the strips of metal and tried to hand them to her. "Here you go."

"This customer wondered if you had room in your class tonight," the woman behind the counter said, obviously speaking to Veronica. "I wanted to check before I process his payment."

"Payment?" Veronica repeated, her eyes never leaving his.

"For your class?" The woman said with a laugh.

"Right." Veronica blinked and forced a smile with those beautiful lips, finally reaching out and grabbing the metal pieces in his hand. "Yes, I have room for one more." She swallowed hard and the blush spread across her cheeks. "Thanks for checking, Steph. Come on back when you're done, Gabe."

Veronica didn't seem happy to see him, but what had he expected? That he'd just show up and say, "Surprise! It's me, the idiot who dumped you twenty years ago. Ready for another go?" She would never forgive him. This was a terrible idea.

"Sign here, then head back to the classroom," the woman said, pulling him out of his thoughts.

It was too late to leave now, so he nodded and followed the direction of her finger where two other women were already wearing safety glasses and listening attentively to whatever Veronica was telling them.

Without preamble, she handed him a piece of paper and continued talking. He signed his name at the bottom and handed it back to her.

"That's a safety waiver. You should read it. Know what you're getting yourself into." Veronica stared at him, a frown creasing her forehead.

"I know what I'm getting into," he said, hoping she understood he wasn't talking about the class. The last time he'd seen her, he'd been a stupid young guy with no plan for the future. She, on the other hand, had a grand future planned. If he'd been smart enough to hold onto her, his life would've been very different.

"Okay," she said as her frown deepened. "Put these on."

She handed him a pair of safety glasses, and that's when he saw the G drawn onto her skin. Heat burned through his chest as the memory surfaced. One night in bed, he'd found every letter of his name in the constellation of freckles covering her body.

A thrill of happiness zinged through him when he noticed she didn't wear a wedding ring.

Veronica cleared her throat. "Tonight, we're going to make a simple, silver ring." She kept her eyes focused on the other two students. "I'm here to guide you, but I want you to do the work. Learn what it feels like to sand, shape, and heat it. But first, you have to find the right size." With that, she produced a container of blue plastic bands and dumped them into a pile in the middle of the table. "It should be snug but not too tricky to get off."

The women across the table from him reached into the heap of plastic and chatted quietly amongst themselves, leaving Veronica's attention on him.

"What finger should I use?" he asked as he spread his hands out on the table. He couldn't help but smile when she licked her lips.

"Um, you could make a thumb ring." She played with the delicate silver band around her own thumb.

"My knuckles are big, so it might be tricky to get off." As he spoke, her breathing sped up, and she absentmindedly started playing with her necklace. A little silver G hung from it. It was the same size and shape as the G on her hand. He grinned. "Is that a G? *My* G?"

Veronica tried to clear her mind, but her proximity to Gabe made it nearly impossible. All she had to do was focus on teaching and stop staring at his mouth. And his hands. Oh god, those talented hands. She tucked her necklace away and stepped backward, bumping into the table with her tools, knocking some of them over.

"Are you okay?" Gabe asked, leaning toward her.

"Yes." No. How would she ever be okay again? He was right there, staring at her with that smile on his lips. She remembered what those lips felt like. Stop it. "Does everyone have their ring size picked out?"

The two women nodded in unison, but Gabe scrambled to find one, which he shoved onto his thumb and promptly grimaced.

"I think it's too small." Panic filled his eyes as he tugged at it. "It won't come off."

Veronica gave him a reassuring smile. "Don't worry, I have a trick that should work. Ladies, I want you to pick the kind of wire you want to use while I help him." She fanned out the stack of wires, which all varied in width.

"Let's go to the utility sink," she said to Gabe, leading him to the other side of the room. "Soap should work."

Gabe followed her and thrust his hand out toward her when they reached the sink. "Thanks for helping me."

"Sure." She pumped some hand soap into her palm and coated his thumb generously, twisting and massaging the slippery liquid all over his digit. He closed his eyes and groaned. It was the same noise he used to make when she wrapped her hand around . . . something else. Her cheeks heated and she stilled her hands. He opened his eyes slowly, looking first at where they were touching, and then to her face. "Sorry," she said, but she didn't pull away from him.

"You have nothing to apologize for. I—"

"What do we do now?" One of the women called out from the classroom.

"Hang on, I'm coming," Veronica said over her shoulder.

"Veronica." Her name came out as a plaintive whisper.

"We can't. Not here. Not now."

With a quick tug, she pulled the ring smoothly off his big knuckle. "You should pick the next size up."

"Whatever you say." After he rinsed and dried his hands, they rejoined the rest of the class and started to work.

Thankfully, talking about her work seemed to break the spell between her and Gabe, and everything became easy again. He was just another student in her class. The only thing that mattered was helping them make rings.

———

Gabe did exactly what he was told, and his ring still looked horrible. He held the lumpy thing in his palm and scowled at it. She had made it look so easy.

"What's wrong?" Veronica asked.

"It looks awful."

"No, it doesn't. I told you it wouldn't be perfect. You can fix it later." She patted his arm in a way that was probably meant to be reassuring, but it only sparked his desire. She plucked the ring out of his hand, dropped it into a bowl with the other three, and addressed the class, "This pickling solution will clean off the oxidized metal from the solder. It will take a few minutes. Feel free to roam through the store, use the bathroom, or grab a snack. See you back here in ten minutes." She set a timer on her phone and turned her back to him while she organized her tools. The other two students disappeared into the store, leaving them alone again.

He stepped up behind her, wishing he could wrap his arms around her. "It's good to see you again, Veronica."

She turned and looked up at him. "It's good to see you

too." Her voice was barely audible. "How did you find me?" She sighed. "I didn't mean for that to sound accusatory. It's just that a lot has happened in twenty years, and I'm not where I was then."

"Did you ever get married?" he blurted out, unable to wait another minute before finding out.

"I did, but it didn't stick." She frowned.

"I'm sorry," he said, and he meant it.

"Are you?" Her frown deepened and she stepped away from him.

That's what she had wanted from him. Marriage, kids, and a house in the suburbs. It had scared him. "I know how much you wanted that. What happened?"

She dropped her shoulders a little. "We were happy for a while, and then we weren't. How about you?"

"No one ever stuck to me, either. Are you seeing anyone?"

"No. You?"

He shook his head and closed the gap between them and took her hand in his, another pulse of pleasure shot through him. "I thought I imagined this."

"What?" She blinked slowly. Could she sense it too?

"The feeling I get when I touch you." It was the same all-consuming need he felt when they first met.

"No one has ever made me feel the way you do." Her soft words made his heart race faster.

"Can I kiss you?"

Veronica nodded and leaned toward him, her breath coming fast and shallow. Gabe lowered his face until their lips were almost touching. That's when her alarm rang.

———

"Shoot," Veronica muttered under her breath as she fumbled to pull her phone out of her back pocket to silence the alarm. How had it already been ten minutes? Time flies when you're trying to make out with your old boyfriend.

With a bright smile plastered on her heated face, she directed her students to their seats so they could get back to work. "Now we quench our rings again," she said as she dropped the rings into water a second time. After her near kiss with Gabe, she wished she had a bowl big enough to quench her entire body. Maybe that would put out the fires he stirred in her. Or, maybe the only way to get him out of her system was to take him home and—stop it.

She had to focus on work, her sanity depended on it. So that's what she did. She distributed their rings and the tools they would need, then she slid her ring onto the tapered mandrel and tapped the ring gently with a rawhide mallet to demonstrate the technique.

"Take your time. This is a slow process." She started with the women first, giving them pointers then leaving them to their work, their backs to Gabe. When she turned her attention on him, she noticed it was hard to think about work when he spoke.

"How am I doing?" Gabe asked, turning his body toward her, holding the ring and mandrel up for her inspection.

"Uh-huh." She wrapped her hand around his. His skin was so warm and smooth.

"Veronica?" A smile played on his lips.

"Huh?" She tore her eyes away from his mouth and met his eyes. "What did you say?"

"How am I doing?"

She looked down at their hands and the ring he'd been working on. "Oh, that. Fine. What are you doing after class?"

she whispered. If she could get him alone for a minute, maybe she'd get a chance to kiss him.

"I planned to apologize for making the biggest mistake of my life."

That stopped her sexy time thoughts. "To me?"

"Of course, to you." He stroked her arm and heat went through her. "I owe you that. And more."

The way he said *more* made her brain mushy. What did it mean? More talking? More kissing? More touching? She hoped it was the latter. "Uh-huh."

Gabe laughed. "How much longer is class?"

She shook her head, trying to clear the fog in her brain and stepped away from him. "An hour." She could wait an hour, couldn't she?

He groaned, the sound filled with need and frustration.

Knowing he was just as wound up as her made her ridiculously happy. "Aren't you having a good time?"

"My idea of a good time doesn't involve an audience," he whispered.

She couldn't stifle the gasp that came out of her mouth, which she quickly covered with a cough. If she could survive the next hour, it would be a miracle.

———

At the end of class, Gabe wrapped his arm around Veronica's waist and followed her out of the building and down the sidewalk. When they turned the corner at the end of the building, Veronica faced him and crushed her lips against his. Surprise quickly gave way to the need he'd kept in check all night. He caressed the sides of her face as Veronica deepened the kiss. He leaned back against the rough brick wall to steady them.

Voices came from farther down the sidewalk, so he pulled away from her mouth and said, "I missed you."

Veronica licked her swollen lips and nodded. "So much."

The other people came closer, talking loudly. Gabe didn't want an audience for what he had to say to her. "Can we go somewhere to talk?"

"My place. I live two blocks away."

They walked briskly to the new apartment complex downtown. Her hands shook as she unlocked the outer door. "Follow me," she said as she ran up a flight of stairs and opened the door to her apartment.

Gabe stepped inside and glanced around the small, neat front room, his eyes landing on Veronica's face. "I'm so sorry I let you go. I was such a fool."

"You were." A smile tugged up the corner of her mouth as she stepped toward him.

Even though he wanted to kiss her again, he took a step away from her. She deserved to know the truth. "I was afraid. I didn't know how to give you what you wanted, so I ran away. That was the worst mistake of my life, and I hope you'll give me another chance."

"I shouldn't have let you leave," she whispered.

"Can you forgive me?" He swallowed hard.

Veronica nodded and stepped toward him. "Yes. Now will you kiss me again?"

He didn't hesitate, and when his mouth met hers, he sighed. She wrapped her arms around his neck and leaned against him. He slid his hands down to her waist and caressed the strip of exposed skin, the motion making her freeze.

"My body has changed a lot in twenty years."

"I've always loved your body. Is this okay?" He trailed a finger across her spine, enjoying every inch of her soft skin.

Veronica closed her eyes and sighed as she nodded, their noses rubbing. "I like the way you touch me."

"You're beautiful." She was softer and fuller than before, the years making her lovelier than ever.

She kissed him again and guided him backward. Something pressed against the backs of his legs, and then they were falling. With Veronica's arms tangled around his neck and his hands pressed against her back, they held onto each other as the couch engulfed them.

"Sorry, I thought that would be more graceful." Veronica laughed and struggled to right herself, only managing to press her body closer to his.

Gabe sputtered a mixture of laughs and groans as she rubbed against him. The contact almost more than he could manage. The sound of their laughter muffled everything, including the noise of someone opening the front door.

"My study group ended early tonight, so I thought I'd surprise you with a *what the*—" The man's voice cut off abruptly as his eyes met Gabe's.

———

Veronica startled at the sound of Henry's voice, and she fell onto the floor with a thud.

"Wow," Henry said.

"It's not what it looks like." Veronica laughed. It was *exactly* what it looked like. She scrambled to her feet and looked at Gabe, who struggled to sit up, his legs bent awkwardly over the end of the couch.

Gabe clenched his jaw, and when he spoke, his words came out low and threatening. "Who are you?"

Henry scoffed. "Who are *you*? I live here."

Hurt slashed through Gabe's features. As if she had

cheated on him. No, not on him. With him. Before she could clear up this mess, Henry opened his mouth.

"Jesus, Mom. Why didn't you text to let me know?"

"Mom?" Gabe frowned.

"Henry, this is Gabe. Gabe, this is my *son*, Henry."

"You have a son?" His mouth hung open.

"Wait, *the* Gabe?" Henry had a small birthday cake in his hands, realization dawning on his face. "I guess he found you, huh?"

Gabe frowned and finally stood up. Veronica lunged to press a small pillow against the fly of Gabe's jeans. Even in the dim lighting, she could see just how excited their make out session had made him.

"He found me."

"I'm thrilled to finally meet you." Henry held the cake in one hand and offered his other to Gabe, but pulled it back almost immediately. "On second thought, I don't know where those hands have been."

"Honey," Veronica scolded.

"Don't pretend you're innocent." Henry smirked.

Gabe stared at Henry, narrowing his eyes. "He's named after your dad, isn't he? He looks just like him. It's uncanny."

"You knew my grandpa?" Henry grinned.

Gabe nodded, and a smile softened the edges of his mouth. "It's like being a teenager again and getting caught by your dad. Talk about déjà vu."

"No one is supposed to catch anyone doing anything. This is why we have a system," Henry said.

"Our system has been one-sided until now. I forgot, okay?" Heat spread across her cheeks.

Henry sighed. "I guess I'll let it slide, but now I'm scarred for life."

"Oh, please." Veronica huffed. "I'm sure you and your therapist are going to have a hay day with this."

A smile broke across Henry's face. "True. Now, if you'll excuse me, I'm going to David's place for the night. Maybe we could all get together for dinner this weekend, as long as you promise to keep your hands to yourself."

Veronica scowled at him.

"Nice to meet you, Gabe. Happy birthday, Mom." He leaned toward her and kissed her cheek, then whispered, "I can totally see the appeal. Have fun tonight."

"Henry!"

He handed her the cake. "Save me a piece?"

"Would you leave already?" Veronica laughed and pushed him out the door. She turned around slowly, biting her bottom lip. "That is not how I wanted you to meet Henry."

———

"You have a son," Gabe repeated, still unable to process everything that had just happened.

"I do. Sorry I forgot to text him."

"He's so like you." Relief and grief battled inside him. He was relieved she had gotten what she wanted most, a family, but mourned the fact that he hadn't been a part of it.

"He and I have always been close. It made Brad jealous, I think."

"Your ex?"

Veronica nodded and tears welled in her eyes. "Brad wanted a family too, so we got married a few months after we met and started trying to get pregnant. I thought he was the perfect man." She shook her head and squeezed her eyes shut, forcing the tears down her cheeks. "He left when Henry came out. How can a father reject his ten-year-old son? I always knew Henry was gay, and I thought Brad did too." She paused and searched his eyes, probably to gauge his reaction. "He said the most hurtful things."

Gabe gathered her into his arms and hugged her. "I think Henry is wonderful. Your dad would've loved him."

She wiped at her cheeks and smiled. "That's what I always say."

"Why didn't you tell me about him?"

Veronica shrugged then put her hands on his chest. "I didn't want him to get hurt again. Plus, it seemed too soon. Like it was too much all at once."

"I'll never hurt him," Gabe said, and she relaxed in his arms. "And if I've learned anything from my past mistakes, it's that there's no such thing as too much at once. I want it all when it comes to you." He stroked the soft skin of her cheek. "I love you, Veronica."

"I love you, Gabe. Always have, always will."

I ONLY READ ROMANCE

LIZ CHRISTENSEN

"I ONLY READ ROMANCE NOVELS," Grace Hart mumbled. She replaced the weathered H.P. Lovecraft on the overburdened bookshelf. Navigating the labyrinthine stacks of Rory's Rare Books was complicated. The disorganized collection was charming for the first fifteen minutes of browsing. But Grace's lunch break was coming to a quick close. If she didn't find the romance section or even a single romance novel soon, she was going back to work at the bakery without a paperback. And without a paperback, she'd have nothing to snuggle up with when she went to bed that night.

My life is so pathetic, Grace moaned mentally.

She tipped the top of a book spine from the shelf as she eyed the title *Best of Elizabeth Barrett Browning*. Close but not what she was looking for.

She decorated wedding cakes all day for Your Cake and Eat It Too bakery. Her entire work life centered around other people finding love. She wanted narrative fiction with a leading man she could dream about.

"Bare-chested types or the ones that wear gloves?"

Grace gasped, knocking the poetry collection she was

fingering from the shelf. A brown eye behind a bifocal frame blinked at her from the other side of the stacks.

"Excuse me?"

"Your type of romance novel." The brown eye stared back. The wrinkles around the eye indicated a hint of a smile and more than a little age. The face repositioned itself, sticking the lips into the narrow space between books. "Do you like the gentleman-type leading man or the Adonis type?"

Grace tucked her hair behind her ear. "Um, either actually."

The brown eye came back, sizing her up and down. It squinted.

"Follow me," came the muffled invitation.

Following the soft footfalls, Grace negotiated the tunnels of bookshelves. And hit a dead end. She checked her watch. Five minutes left to get a book and go back to work. She'd have to bail.

Grace made an about-face only to see a man backlit by the shop windows at the other end of the aisle. Dust flickered in the streaming light pouring around him. He had a cane, but whether it was for character or stability, Grace couldn't tell. He was wearing eyeglasses. They were the only thing in his silhouette which caught an occasional glint of light.

He raised his cane at her like a sword. "Second shelf from the top, over your left shoulder, third book from the end, if you read left to right, which you do. Titled *Eternal Encounter*."

Grace followed the instructions. She found the small, hardbound book covered in faded jade. The gold embossed letters of the title and author were waning. The author's name was indecipherable. Grace guessed the book was likely a century old.

Time was up. It was this book or she left empty-handed.

"Perfect. I'll take it. How much?" she asked, turning the

book around, opening the front cover and not finding any price mark.

"You're in a hurry. You can set the bill in your right jacket pocket on the shelf and get going."

Grace remembered the five dollars she had in change from picking up her bagel. She retrieved it from her jacket pocket. Had the old man been spying on her? She placed the money in the vacant space created by her removal of *Eternal Encounter*. The adjacent books slid, creating a protective lean-to for her payment.

"Just here?" she asked, casting her eyes back down the aisle. The man was gone. The dust particles floated undisturbed in their ethereal suspension in the sunshine.

Grace left Rory's Rare Books at a quickening pace.

Eternal Encounter bided the time in her over-the-shoulder messenger bag. It dangled from a hook in the back kitchen all afternoon with Grace's jacket. She forgot about the book as she worked on her immaculate frosting flowers. Any cake decorator could do rose buds. A beginner could learn to turn out decent blooming roses, but Grace was no beginner. If a bride or groom would accept fondant, a whole new realm of flower possibilities were on the table.

Grace didn't like the taste of fondant. In Paonia, Colorado, Your Cake and Eat It Too was the only bakery that offered to create any flower with royal or buttercream frosting. If you could have it in your wedding bouquet, you could eat it on your cake. And Grace was the reason why Your Cake and Eat It Too could make and keep that promise.

She finished placing the Persian blue buttercream irises before clocking out. Grace circled the pearl-colored, three-tier masterpiece with caution. Satisfied that it was striking from every angle and therefore finished, Grace washed her hands and hung up her apron. The food coloring mix to create

Persian blue buttercream frosting stained her cuticles. No biggie. She wasn't going out or anything. Remembering her book in the messenger bag brought her some comfort. She'd still have a date night, even if it was pitiful. Her date with the strange find from Rory's Rare Books would be a night in, and she could look however she wanted.

The romantic evening with *Eternal Encounter* began on the couch. Grace had heated up leftover chili from Sunday and was eating it with two pieces of plain, white bread. She leaned her neck back against the armrest. Then, she positioned the bowl of chili and the slices of bread on her stomach. Finally, she rested the spine of the jade-colored hardback cover on her knees. Her feet burrowed between the couch cushions.

Grace was a fast reader. She was three chapters into the novel by the time her dinner was finished. There were some bread crumbs on her chest and a little stain of chili in the corner of her mouth. Some flour had settled on her hair at work, giving her wispy, messy bun a dusted glow. Her lips parted as her eyes devoured line after line. She chewed on the inside of her cheek as the hero of the novel met his leading lady. He was of inherited wealth, an only child with an ailing but estranged father. As a leading man, Robert possessed natural charm, an American Edwardian darling. The first in his storyworld to own a motor car, he loved to go zipping through the country. Easy-going and affable, he was immediately attracted to the vibrant and opinionated ingenue.

Laralee was a young woman of depth and passion. She was homespun, of little means, and the youngest in a large, happy family.

Grace was captivated by them both. Her blue-stained fingertips seized each page.

When Robert embarrassed himself in front of Laralee at

their first meeting, Grace gasped. "Oh no, Robert, not like that. She'll think poorly of you."

Grace furrowed her brow and began to bite at one of her blue-stained cuticles.

"Oh, Laralee, he's not really like that," she chided.

And that was the point in the story that Robert realized—there was a Reader.

He began to observe her as she read about him. How she gripped the book when he was succeeding and slunk deeper into the couch as he made mistakes. It was still early in the story; Robert had quite a few more mistakes to go. But the gaze of this Reader was enticing. Robert played out the motions of his story with his signature nervous infatuation. He contrived his picnic with Laralee. Again he gave a shallow impression of himself.

His Reader moaned and gazed open-mouthed at the ceiling.

Robert could feel her ache for him as his book pressed into her lap. Normally, by now, the Reader believed Robert would never be good enough for Laralee. Time to introduce Calvin, Robert's new rival for her affections. Robert would start succeeding soon, but Calvin and Laralee had a long friendship. It would take Robert chapters to catch up.

But this Reader was still firmly on Robert's side. He wouldn't have to win her back.

He blushed at her loyalty.

Grace's phone rang. She rested the book open-faced against her chest as she answered her cell. Robert was overwhelmed with Grace's scent—sugar and vanilla. She smelled like the bakery window display where his motor car would break down nine chapters from now. The bakery would be his turning point. It couldn't be a coincidence. Grace smelled like his redemption. The pages were muffled into her chest. The backdrop of Grace's heartbeat and breathing hypnotized Robert. But he still picked up snatches of her phone call.

It was clear to him that Grace was a shop girl. Robert's money was from department stores. They had something in common. *How charming.* The girl on the other end of the line was asking Grace to take her shift the next day. Grace agreed to cover. Of course the Reader's name was Grace. Impossible she could be named anything else.

Her finger as a placeholder, Grace toted *Eternal Encounter* to the bathroom. She read ten more chapters soaking in the tub. Robert could smell rose petals and vanilla. He adored the way Grace played with the bubbles in the water. She placed some on the tip of her own nose when Robert and Laralee got a bit silly with Laralee's nieces and nephews on Christmas Eve in chapter fourteen. And she kept coaching him and encouraging him.

"Robert, you're clever. Just show her you can make something of yourself."

"Show her how you care for your father. You need to reconcile anyway."

"Ugh, Laralee, Calvin is not the man you want. You're just an adornment to him. It's Robert who values your independence and sees you the way you are."

In all his years in fiction, Robert had never felt so understood, so appreciated, so seen.

Grace finally put *Eternal Encounter* down at her bedside. Robert mulled things over. She had used a small sock as a bookmark. It was pink, fuzzy, and a little worn. It smelled like sugary citrus blossoms. It made it impossible for the book to properly close. Robert was dizzy with thoughts, scents, and sounds reminding him of Grace all night. She slept sprawled out flat on her stomach, one arm splayed wide across the bed. Her other arm curled her pillow up underneath her cheek.

There were watercolor paintings tacked up all over the walls, fluttering with each pass of Grace's rotating fan. The collection included birds, sunsets, flowers, trees, and cottages. Robert was certain Grace had painted them.

She was a romantic, like he was. She saw everything in full color, like he did. Grace surrendered herself to idyllic notions. She was perceptive of details. Her hand seemed patient and steady. Her appreciation seemed forgiving and her talents able.

By the time Grace put *Eternal Encounter* in her messenger bag to head to work the next day, Robert was completely in love with her.

The pink sock still holding place, Robert listened to the music of Grace's morning. She hummed while eggs sizzled in the pan. She made tiny popping sounds with her lips while she waited for her coffee. She tapped the toes of her sneakers like a percussionist even when her earbuds weren't in. Her greetings upon arriving at Your Cake and Eat It Too were like a melody line of jaunty optimism.

Robert watched her work all morning from his spot dangling from Grace's hook on the kitchen wall. There were multiple cakes to complete by the end of the day. Grace had to supervise the work of a junior artist while completing her own masterpiece. Robert had never seen a cake with such vibrant hues. The five tiers were a rich navy blue. Grace added deep red roses, bright sunflowers, orange tulips, and violet chrysanthemums throughout the day. And as she worked, she told her junior about Robert.

"He's dashing, of course, but in a boyish way, with unruly brown curls and a playfulness in his chocolate eyes."

Robert blushed. The book never said his eyes were chocolate. But he liked that she described them like her work— sugary, rich, and delicious.

"He's lived a nonchalant life. Never had to worry about

anything. Then Laralee comes along and stirs something in him. He fights for her by fighting for himself. He's doing all these things he never cared about, and he's finding all this sincerity and depth in himself. Now he's about to lose her to Calvin, and he's such a man that he won't stand in the way. I just can't wait until she sees what he's become. She's being so pig-headed and stubborn. I do like her, though, the way he thinks about her and describes her. I'd hate her in real life because I'd never measure up to her, but I love her for his sake. This book better end with them in each other's arms, or I'm going to be so pissed." Grace laughed, and Robert sighed.

On her lunch break, Grace slipped her pink sock out of *Eternal Encounter*. She held the place with her finger and towed Robert to a coffee shop across the street. Hungry for the novel, she ordered only a croissant and a hot chocolate. Grace and her book sat together at a sidewalk table for two and adored each other for the next twenty-three minutes.

"We had a customer leave without their order this morning. You want it, Grace?" A man with a green apron and blond hair pulled back in a bun asked. He held out a square, flaky creation of cheese and herbs on a small white napkin.

What sort of fellow is this? Robert scoffed. *Hair done up like a sloppy, old maid's. If he hadn't a beard, I wouldn't have known he was a man at all.*

"Thanks Daniel." Grace glanced up from her novel.

"Good book?" he asked.

Why do you linger? Robert accused. *Get back to your shop, lad. The lady has company already.*

"It's sweet and charming. I'm sure I know how it'll end, but it's really lovely and fresh anyway." Grace smiled as she turned to look up at Daniel.

No, no. Come back to the book, Grace. Come back to me, Robert pleaded.

"Have you read anything by Georgette Heyer?" Daniel asked.

Grace placed *Eternal Encounter* face down on the table.

"I love Georgette Heyer. Have you read anything by Elizabeth Gaskell?" Grace asked.

"North and South," Daniel said.

There was a bit of silence. Robert craned his neck and twisted, but he couldn't see anything.

"Well . . ." Daniel began.

"Ah, my break is up." Grace snatched Robert from the table and hugged him with one arm to her chest. She didn't even mark her place.

"See you later, Grace," Daniel called as she dashed back across the street.

Robert stewed in the messenger bag all afternoon. He couldn't see Grace, he couldn't hear her, and he couldn't stop thinking about her. And at the rate she was reading, he only had one night left with her.

Grace ordered pizza delivery that night. She only got through a slice and a quarter before she set the pizza down to read with both hands on the novel. She sat on the floor in front of her couch.

When Laralee decided Calvin wasn't for her, Grace had to move. She lay on the couch with her knees over the backrest and her hair brushing the floor.

Then, Robert and Laralee had a chance private conversation during the concert party. Grace sat cross-legged on the middle cushion, chewing her cuticles.

Robert's big speech was coming up. It would win Laralee's heart for good, though the leading lady wouldn't realize it until the next morning. Then the denouement. Laralee would make a bold and dashing chase after Robert, confess her love to him, and they would kiss. *Eternal Encounter* would end a few paragraphs later. Robert wasn't ready for Grace to say goodbye. But a Reader like Grace never stopped after the concert party. If they'd stuck with Robert and Laralee this long, they knew happiness was coming soon. They knew Laralee wouldn't let Robert go now. They'd read on until she had him.

Laralee waited under the lanterns dangling from the big maple tree in the garden. Robert did what he always did, and asked to speak with her.

The conversation was hesitant at first, as it was written to be. It gave Robert time to think. He studied Grace reading him. She was hooked, no surprise there. But her eyes were watering a little. Robert wondered if she'd gotten flour in her eyes during the afternoon at the bakery. Maybe she had allergies.

It was the part before his confession. Robert began to tell Laralee the kind of woman she was. He felt like he was saying these words for the first time. And they were all about Grace.

"You move through life with all the passion and persistence of a firework. You burn beautifully. What a bang you make. You dazzle, you sizzle. And then you push me away, afraid I'll see the vapor of smoke and darkness following fast. You underestimate yourself, my dear. You are not only a crack of brilliance fading quickly into the sky. You astound me. I close my eyes, and you explode again and again against my eyelids. Echoes of you dot my vision, and you ring in my ears. I cannot make you love me. I cannot keep you at my side. But you make me want to take on the world. You make me want to burst with the best and brightest I have. You burn into my soul. I am enamored of you. I love you," Robert swallowed, "Laralee."

The word felt wrong.

"And so I will respect what you ask of me. Tomorrow, I will leave you and never trouble you again. But I will leave you a changed man and a better man, I hope. And for that, you will always burn brightly to me."

The tears that drifted down Grace's cheeks and clung to her chin pierced Robert to the center. She wasn't crying for the beauty of his words nor for the false despair that Laralee would lose her Robert. Grace pressed *Eternal Encounter* to her chest and sniffled.

Two teardrops abandoned her chin and splashed on the jade-colored spine. They seeped into the book. Robert tasted the salt of Grace's tears. He read the beating of her heart. He heard the uneven breathing in her chest, and he knew. Grace didn't believe she was a firework. She didn't believe she could burn in someone else's heart and soul. Grace had no idea she was a leading lady.

She cried for a while. When she finished, she closed *Eternal Encounter* without a bookmark. Robert spent a dark night on the coffee table wondering if Grace would ever give him a chance to try that speech again. He wanted to make her believe. He wanted her to see. This wasn't about Laralee. Those words were for Grace. She burned in his soul. But Robert had no idea how to prove it to her. He'd spent his best words already. Laralee had a short speech, and the kiss was written in a lovely bit of prose, but that was it. He'd had his chance to adore his lady, to make her feel his fervor, and he'd failed.

Grace woke with a headache. Crying before bedtime always gave her a sadness hangover. She drank some tea and ate a few pieces of bacon, but she didn't have an appetite. The morning was overcast without the promise of rain. Grace grabbed a long knit cardigan on her way out the door. She spotted *Eternal Encounter* on the coffee table. She put it in her messenger bag, not convinced she would read the rest of it.

Robert deserved his happy ending, though, even if Grace was never going to find her own.

Most of the morning was spent deep-cleaning the kitchen. Grace ordered ingredients and supervised the stocking and organizing of the supplies. Your Cake and Eat It Too had a break in orders. On her way to lunch, Grace got approval to decorate a new three-tiered styrofoam structure for the display window. She grabbed her messenger bag thinking more about the sketch paper and the pencil inside than about the novel.

Grace pulled her cardigan tight around her and folded her arms, trapping it in place. None of her thumbnail sketches struck her fancy quite right. She thought about the shop window in *Eternal Encounter*.

No. That wouldn't do it.

The field of wildflowers where Robert and Laralee had their ill-fated picnic. Grace reached into her bag, and withdrew the hardback. She flipped through the book until she found the brief description of the scenery. It was a field that looked like a spill of colored-pencil shavings. She didn't want her flowers backed by green for this cake display, she wanted golden straw. Grace left the book open, face up on the table, the pages turning with an occasional breeze.

Robert stared at his beloved Reader. Conviction, passion, and enthusiasm painted across her face as she worked at her design. Robert would never be able to make Grace feel that way about herself. No one could make anyone feel that way. Laralee had taught him that.

As the pages of his story wafted by him, Robert remembered: Laralee didn't change him; Robert changed himself. She had inspired him. If only Robert could inspire Grace the same way. If he could, if his love could send her with renewed energy in the right direction, that would be enough.

Robert skimmed over his story as the pages of *Eternal*

Encounter lilted in the gentle wind. How could he help Grace see what she could make of herself if reading his story hadn't shown her? How could he open her eyes to her personal possibilities?

Grace sketched her ideas for the wildflower field window display with bold strokes. Her lunch order lay completely untouched beside her. Her nose turned red, and she sniffled against the cold of the day. Her fingers held a commanding grasp on her pencil that would not be deterred or distracted.

Daniel approached from behind, a book tucked in his arms, but Grace didn't notice.

Robert did. He watched Daniel shuffle the book from one hand to the other, his eyes darting from Grace to her sketch.

Daniel licked his lips and swallowed.

Grace was consumed by her task.

Daniel shifted his feet and looked back at his coffee shop.

Robert knew Daniel was going to go back inside and leave Grace to her enthrallment. She leaned closer to her sketch, sliding her elbow along the table in her excited absorption. Daniel began to turn away. And Robert launched himself at the turning of a page. *Eternal Encounter* slid off the table to the pavement.

Grace and Daniel both reached for the book, but Daniel got there first.

"Thanks!" Grace smiled as Daniel placed the closed novel back on the cafe table. She glanced at Daniel's hands. "Whatcha got there?" She pointed with her eraser at the hardback book Daniel had brought out from the shop with him.

"It's a . . ." He handled the book back and forth, then set it on the table as well, nudging *Eternal Encounter* a few inches away. "It's a copy of *The Black Moth* by Georgette Heyer. It was her first real work, so most people aren't as familiar with it."

Grace looked up from her sketch. Her eyes ran over the

book, then up to Daniel. She placed her writing hand on the table and leaned back in her chair.

"I've never read it," she admitted.

"Neither have I," Daniel confessed, "but the bookseller recommended it."

Grace smiled and then pulled her lips back to a forced neutral.

"But maybe you could let me know what you think of it," Daniel finished. He put both his hands in his back pockets and raised his shoulders up to his ears.

"It's for me?" Grace set down her pencil and reached a tentative hand to the book. Daniel nodded. She picked it up and thumbed the pages. Then, she closed *The Black Moth* and set it on top of *Eternal Encounter*. She slid both books closer to her with a gesture that invited Daniel to take the chair across from her at the table. He did.

"You always have a romance novel here at lunch, so I figured you must like them."

"I do." Grace laughed, then pressed her mouth closed. She tucked a wisp of hair behind her ear. "I thought you were a fan of them too. Elizabeth Gaskell and whatnot."

Daniel shrugged, his cheeks flashing more pink than his cold nose. He clasped his hands and buried them in his apron as he leaned forward. "I've only done the research lately. To see if I could have something to talk with you about." He winced at his own honesty, and Grace looked back at Your Cake and Eat It Too across the street for no reason at all.

Both employees took liberties with their lunch breaks that day, though nothing terrible came of it. In fact, something rather sweet and warm came of it. It turned out Grace and Daniel could find plenty of things to talk about. That day they talked about Grace's ideas for the wildflower field cake design in the bakery window. They laughed at the antics of Daniel's

Jack Russell. They discovered their mutual interest in the *Elder Scrolls* video games.

Grace finished both *Eternal Encounter* and *The Black Moth* but not right away. She kept finding other things she wanted to do. She made plans, sometimes with Daniel, sometimes without. She framed some of her watercolors and began to display them in places other than her bedroom. A few went up on the walls of Your Cake and Eat It Too, a few on the walls of the coffee shop across the street.

A couple months later, Grace was taking a brisk walk on her lunch break, her ankle-high boots sloshing through the melt of winter on the sidewalk. She'd developed a habit of analyzing window displays in the storefronts of Paonia. She'd set a goal to do the same with exercise. Whenever Daniel's lunch break didn't line up with hers, she'd spend the entire thirty minutes on the go.

With only eight minutes left in her break, Grace found herself outside Rory's Rare Books. The view through the windows was as cluttered as the aisles inside, as haphazard in arrangement. Grace began to scheme her own ideas for how to decorate the windows, when she noticed her own reflection.

Her messy bun had started to fall, slouching to the side. There was a smudge of flour on the underside of her chin and some red frosting streaked above her left eyebrow. Her cheeks were flushed with the heat of her walk against the cold of early spring. Grace smiled at herself and the romantic notion that captured her thoughts. She was so much like the book store. A little messy in the appearance, but wonderful surprises lay on the inside.

With that, she pranced back to the bakery, bursting with an idea she couldn't wait to try. Flower-shaped frosting was revealed inside the cake with each slice. Grace was inspired, ready to take on new worlds. She pulsed with the energy of months spent believing she could burn bright.

Exploding with her new idea, Grace mused, *Daniel will be so proud.*

Robert would be too.

THE COLONEL

BRYAN YOUNG

"Hey, man, you don't talk to the Colonel. You listen to him. . . .
He's a poet warrior in the classic sense."
– Dennis Hopper as The Photojournalist, *Apocalypse Now*

THE COLONEL WAS A TERRIBLY polite fellow and, perhaps, the greatest rockabilly bluegrass singer I'd ever seen perform live. He'd pour so much soul and scream into his voice that every show he played would surely be his last. His shows were so high energy that they all, invariably, ended with him dangling his almost emaciated frame from the rafters, singing into an old fashioned microphone, dripping sweat from every pore. In most bands, the drummer set the pace, but in this case, the Colonel did.

But as nice as he was and as incredible as his shows were, you couldn't leave him alone for five minutes with your girl.

The night I learned this hard lesson came on the heels of a night that would've been unforgettable on its own. It began as many evenings for many people do: I picked her up at 7:00.

The *her* in question was a beautiful, young girl named Katherine, and I had eyes only for her.

I drove us to dinner before the show, where we both ordered blueberry hefeweizens with our meals.

We talked of this and that, of books, and movies, and little things in each other's lives, as we often did, but when the conversation came around to us, my heart leapt in my chest. "We" were my favorite subject. Who doesn't like hearing about what a pretty girl thinks of *us*?

But I was never the best at expressing myself, cursed forever to send mixed or confusing signals.

"If you like me so much," she asked, a confused pause in her cadence, "why has love never once come up?"

I furrowed my brow, twice as confused as she appeared to be. "Are you serious?"

The blank stare on her milky, freckled face and the still bob of her curled hair that had escaped her top bun told me she was completely in earnest. She puckered her lips and looked left and right, trying hard to remember anything that had been talked about previously.

Then, she shook her head, shyly, sheepishly.

"Literally the last time we were out, that happened." I took a long gulp of the tart beer and set the mug back down on the table, harder than I'd intended.

Her shining brown eyes darted back and forth as she held her breath, rifling through her memory, searching for that shred of an event she'd clearly missed.

I drew in a sharp breath of my own that pulled with an airy weight that tugged down at my heart. It hadn't occurred to me that I would have to set the scene all over again. "We'd gone to see a movie, then ended up at the restaurant, drinking. I stopped at one, knowing I'd have to drive, and you kept going as we talked . . ."

"We talked about my mother and my brother-in-law."

"And the movie. And politics. And that Graham Greene

book I lent you. Which led to us moving to the coffee shop for you to sober up."

"Did we?"

"I bought you a vanilla latte, and we walked out back, and you collapsed on the grass strip by the parking lot."

"Okay, I remember all that."

"And we laid in the grass. And we talked about that book until it turned into talk about us. Then, I read you that awful thing I'd written you."

"The poem?"

"Staring up at the stars, laying there on the grass, I recited a poem I'd written. A terrible poem. About you. And you seemed very overwhelmed. You turned your head to me, looked at me, right into me with the starlight sparkling in your eyes and took a deep breath that came with a smile. A beautiful, contented, loving smile."

She smiled again at this description, flushed with embarrassment. "You really do think in movies, don't you?"

I nodded, half smiling. "Maybe. But there we were, looking into each other's eyes, drunk on beer, moonlight, and each other, and I whispered lowly, 'I love you.'"

Not one iota of confusion left her face. If anything, she added a patina of hurt to the look. "I don't . . ."

"At that point, you smiled and whispered back, 'I love you too,' and I wanted to kiss you so badly I ached. And you don't remember any of that, do you?"

"I didn't think I was that drunk . . ."

"Me neither." I sighed.

With both hands, she raised her beer mug to her lips, obscuring her eyes and face.

The deflation her faulty memory caused was equally bolstered by the fact that she finally knew how I felt and couldn't deny it.

I sighed and looked down into my beer, wondering if I'd missed a signal or interpreted something incorrectly. If she wasn't comfortable with how I felt and didn't reciprocate those feelings, why did she keep agreeing to date me?

The slow dance around our relationship boggled my mind, doubly so when it stopped to listen to the sexually charged and breakneck speed of the music we waltzed our friendship around to.

Talk drifted to the show we were to attend and excitement to see the Colonel and his beer band rock the roof off the Bar Named Sue.

Soon enough, with hearts confused and heavy but cruising for a good time, we entered the old, stained, wooden door of the bar. As we stepped inside, holding hands, the growing stench of booze and fading smell of weed met us head on. The bouncer took our IDs with a grunt, sliding his sleeve up and checking the underside of his forearm, as though it held, for some reason, the permission for us to enter.

He waved us by, and we came into the crowd. Music lovers of all shapes and sizes packed the room, shoulder to shoulder. Most held bottles of cheap beer or cans of even cheaper Pabst Blue Ribbon. The fashion of the crowd was divided evenly between the rockabilly enthusiasts dressed like some variation of The Stray Cats, all ready to swing, and the other half of us dressed in street clothes, just there to enjoy the music.

The show wouldn't start for a while yet. The sun was still too high in the sky, so Katherine and I took our place at the bar and ordered more beer.

"Want a sidecar?" the bartender asked us both.

I turned to her. "Want a shot of anything?"

"Sure." The edges of her mouth curled into a sly smile that warmed me.

"Jameson's," I told the bartender, who produced our drinks quickly enough.

Swiveling on the barstools, we turned our backs from the bar to face the stage and dance floor. Not that much dancing would be possible. By the time the show started, the floor would be packed. Why the Colonel didn't play shows at bigger venues was beyond me, but it worked to my advantage. At my best, I could only handle about a bar full of people in one place at one time.

Katherine didn't care.

Why would she? She was the prettiest girl in any room of any size.

A man took the stage, a beefy gentleman in a flannel shirt and elevator shoes, carrying an old electric guitar. His hair was greased into a perfect pompadour, and it wasn't until we looked closer that we could see that he was probably twice as old as the rest of the crowd.

Rock and roll knew no age.

The middle-aged rocker slung the guitar around his shoulder and leaned down into the microphone. His band-mates filled in behind him, taking their places at the drums and the bass. "Hey, we're the Unlucky Boys, and we're gonna play a few songs for you."

The bass player thumped, and the drummer slammed, and the guitarist rocked a chord, and they played fast tunes about truck driving and losing the girl. And they were a perfect warm up for a man like the Colonel. They pumped up the crowd that continued to stagger in through the door a few at a time.

By the time the Unlucky Boys had finished their fourth song, the dance floor was packed, and the place was ready for a religious experience.

"You excited?" I yelled into Katherine's ear at a distance that should've required a whisper.

"Of course," she said before taking another long draught from her beer.

The more I drank, the more I felt like I was floating, especially when I was around her. When she lowered the stein of beer from her face, my eyes caught hers twinkling in the spotlights of the bar.

I don't know how long the Unlucky Boys played, but I hardly saw them. By the time they'd finished their set, I realized I'd spent the whole time stealing glances at Katherine. Who could blame me?

The Unlucky Boys cleared the stage, and we had finished our drinks. I ordered us another round and waited for the moment the Colonel would take the stage and transcend time and space to blow the roof off the venue.

"I'm going to the little girls' room," Katherine said after a time, putting her stein back on the bar.

I replied with a smile and watched her walk away toward the back of the bar where the restrooms were.

Alone, with no band on the stage, I was able to talk myself into talking to her. I knew I needed to tell her exactly how I felt and what I wanted.

I wanted to kiss her. I wanted to kiss her so badly it made my lips and my heart ache. And watching her walk away, and knowing she'd have to do that same walk when I dropped her off at home, killed me. But it doubled my resolve. I'd try to kiss her tonight.

In all the time we'd spent together, in all the time we'd talked, and in all the times we'd gone out, we'd never kissed.

We'd hugged. We'd breathed heavily on each other's necks. We'd nibbled on ears. But to that point we'd never kissed. That had seemed like something special we had to wait for.

And I knew I was going to try that night.

If she refused me, that would be okay. I'd be silently heart-broken, but we'd still be friends. And I'd still love her even if we couldn't be lovers. I'd end the confusion once and for all and tell her what I hoped and dreamed for the two of us.

But who knows what happens with the best laid plans of mice and men?

She came back and must have noticed that I wore a smile on my face like a guilty plea. Did she know what I'd resolved to do? Did she know how happy it made me? "What's that smile for, soldier?" she asked.

With the alcohol doing my thinking for me, I leaned in close to her, my lips almost brushing against her ear. "I'm just really goddamn happy to be here with you."

I resisted the urge to kiss her on the neck and leaned back to see an irrepressible smile on her face as well. It was conta-gious, and I smiled even wider.

She leaned in to the side of my head, getting just as close to me as I'd gotten to her. Her breath on my ear caused a shiver up my spine. Then she spoke: "I'm really happy to be here with you too."

I almost melted.

Could you blame me?

We did this back and forth, having a conversation in this manner. It was a good way to go crazy, holding back every-thing when you just wanted to brush a finger along her cheek and bring her face closer until your lips met.

But that needed a more private, perfect moment.

Knowing that didn't make that yearning ache any less prevalent, though.

And besides, the show was about to start.

The Colonel took the stage slowly. The lights dimmed for him, and the crowd hushed. Many of them knew what they were in for; the rest just followed their lead. They'd heard stories about the Colonel. *Everyone* had heard stories about the Colonel.

The spotlight activated, pouring bright, white light on the man, bringing every feature into detail. He was wiry, a stick frame of a man beneath his button-up shirt and blue jeans. His hair was dark at the roots and lightened up to an almost blond pompadour. His jaw was neatly lined with sideburns that came down and made a right turn toward his mouth. There were marks on his nose where his glasses sat when he wasn't on stage.

He didn't need to see while he was up there.

All he had to do was pour his soul into his microphone.

And even that microphone was special. It was an old Shure Unidyne, a bulky mic the size of an Idaho potato, plated in a worn, chrome skeleton. His voice coming through that receiver was the sort of thing that changed lives.

And maybe it changed mine that night, though I still wonder if it was for better or worse.

"How you fine folks doin' tonight?" He asked in his pleasant Kentucky drawl, some mix between Elvis and a punk-rocker.

The crowd roared and clapped.

"That's just great. Happy to hear it. Well, we're here to play you some music, and I'll be damned if we don't. So how about we get to it?"

The Colonel raised his hand and held it there high in the air. Every eye in the room was transfixed by it. Because when it came down, so too would the house. Such was the power the Colonel held in that moment.

His hand fell, and bedlam began with the strike of his guitar. The first song was fast, and he screamed into that microphone, and the crowd lost its mind. Partway through, the microphone found itself affixed to a stand in front of him, and he'd produced a harmonica. And he blew through that thing with so much soul that I wondered if he'd have any part of his soul left to sell the devil.

That first song ended, and the crowd exploded. The applause from the onlookers prior to that point had been polite and firm, but this was like fireworks accompanied by hooting and hollering.

The Colonel unslung his guitar and managed to take his whole shirt off along with it, revealing the muscled wireframe beneath it.

Three songs later, he was glistening in sweat and hanging from the rafters above the stage like Spider-Man.

It was unbelievable.

The Colonel and his men played two full encores, where I couldn't even imagine they'd have the energy to play one. But those numbers were played with the same forceful vigor as the first song of their set.

After they took their final bow, at least a fourth of the crowd fled, giving everyone left at least a little bit of elbow room. And I suppose that's when Katherine saw an opening.

"I want to go meet him. He seems just amazing."

Being too shy myself, I nodded. "Why don't you go ahead and say hello. I'll close out the tab. Then we'll go?"

She smiled at me. "Deal."

Sliding off her barstool, she made her way into the crowd and toward the stage. For my part, I swiveled around and raised a finger to the bartender.

"Ready to close out?" they asked.

"Yup."

"Alrighty."

The bartender turned back to the cash register and pushed

the buttons on their screen and found the list of drinks Katherine and I had ordered.

It was a long list. Probably a lot longer than it should have been.

We were both pretty tipsy, to say the least. But we weren't irresponsible, trust me. We're not drunk drivers, and I totally had a plan to deal with that. We were going to walk to my office not far from the venue and sober up for however long it took and then come back for the car.

Bearing a receipt as long as my arm, the bartender shoved it, my credit card, and a pen across the bar. The cost of drinks was more than twice the cost of our dinner, but it didn't matter. We were having fun, and that's all I cared about. The money was immaterial.

I added a nice tip to the receipt but found it troublesome to do the math, even the simple addition to add the subtotal and the tip. Fudging the numbers, I scribbled a signature across the paper and slid it back across the bar and thanked the bartender in a voice far more elevated in volume than I'd intended.

Turning back to the dance floor, I saw the crowd was dissipating even faster than before, but at the center of the floor, almost as if the spotlight were on them, were Katherine and the Colonel.

The smile she wore was the smile she'd been giving me all night. And there the Colonel stood, accepting her smile, his shirt only half returned to his body. It was unbuttoned, exposing his bare chest, still heaving up and down as he tried to catch his breath from all the effort of the show.

They spoke, though I couldn't hear the words they said.

She closed her arms in front of her, fidgeting with her hands. Then, she kicked up a leg to toe the floor, staring sheepishly at him with her bottom lip bitten like a schoolgirl with a crush.

And who could fault her for being attracted to a man as talented and handsome as the Colonel?

But it was time for us to go. Sliding off the barstool, I took a step that might have seemed more like a stagger toward them. Then another.

But I was given pause, wondering what was happening when she offered him her right hand and he took it in his hand. He held it delicately and brought it to his lips, kissing the tops of her fingers.

She giggled.

My brow tightened, and confusion grew within me.

This wasn't how things were supposed to go. And this was just the beginning of my hard series of lessons about the man called the Colonel.

When he brought her hand to his bare chest, about the last thing I expected was for Katherine to take a step closer and tilt her head up. And then, when he brought his head down, I never imagined that Katherine's lips would've met his.

A stinging grew in my chest, and my eyes watered. I'd hoped that her lips would meet mine.

Their kiss was sloppy. They were both drunk.

The Colonel had spent the spaces in between the songs of his set drinking. Of course he was drunk. And I knew how drunk Katherine was. And though they were thusly uninhibited by spirits, it was still a surprise to me when they both paused for a breath and the Colonel took Katherine by the hand and led her in the opposite direction.

My heart sank, drowning in confusion.

I couldn't move.

I was paralyzed. I'm still shocked I didn't crumble to the floor, fainting like a goddamned idiot.

What in the hell was going on?

The Colonel brought her to a room I didn't even realize

existed on the side of the stage. I wondered if it was some sort of green room, but this was just a bar. It was probably a storage closet of some kind. Glancing into the crack of the door as the Colonel closed it behind him and Katherine, I could see it was full of all kinds of boxes and cases sized for musical instruments.

Indeed.

The Colonel had dragged my date into a storage closet.

To do who knows what.

I hadn't even realized that I'd covered my mouth with an open palm to disguise my shock.

How does one handle a situation like that? Clearly, she wanted to go with him. She'd commented through the night how handsome and attractive he was (though she'd commented how handsome and attractive I was too). There was no coercion. Did I simply stroll up, knock on the door, and ask for my girl back?

Was she my girl?

I loved her, but I don't suppose that made her *my* girl. She was *her* girl. And she was doing what she wanted to do, even if it hurt me.

I'm not sure how long I spent standing there, deciding on a course of action, but the entire establishment was mostly empty by the time I decided to just turn to the bar and drink until Katherine was ready to go.

Handing my credit card back to the bartender, I ordered a shot of Jameson.

Slugging it back, I ordered another beer that I may or may not have wanted to cry into. Every so often, I would turn back to the doorway, hoping that she would emerge and that we would run away together. But whatever it was she was doing with the Colonel was far more interesting than any time she could have spent with me.

Maybe they were just talking. It was too loud in the bar with the bartender's iPod blaring through the speakers. And a rocker as loud as the Colonel was surely deaf, so any meaningful conversation would have to happen in a quiet place.

Yeah. That was the ticket.

They were just talking.

Sitting there, hunched over the bar like a drunk in an old movie, kidding myself to no end, I sipped my way through that entire beer before the bar made the last call. Closing out my tab again, I found it even harder than before to scrawl my signature on the receipt that seemed suddenly far too tiny for the purpose.

I felt a hand reach up onto my shoulder, and I imagined it was a bouncer trying to kick me out. Or one of the Colonel's roadies to teach me a lesson for bringing so beautiful a girl to a bar and expecting to leave with her still.

I'd already been punched in the heart. Why not in the mouth too?

I tried spinning on the stool toward the direction the hand came from, but there was no one there. Just an empty barstool and no one else around. Looking closer at my right shoulder, I could see fingertips, so I knew someone must've been there. I kept spinning around until I saw Katherine there. She never took her hand off me, so it slid across my chest and planted itself on my left shoulder.

She was close to me.

Closer than I would have expected given the turn the evening had taken.

"Katherine. What the hell happened?" I hiccoughed.

"Are you ready to go?"

"I've been ready to go for . . . I don't know how long. A while. I've been ready to go for a while."

I stood quickly, and all the alcohol rushed straight to my

brain. Dizzied, I almost didn't realize that Katherine had caught me in her arms. My arms wrapped around her, and we held each other in an awkward, drunken embrace.

I heard a snit of breath on my neck, and I knew she'd smiled. "We have to go, Michael."

"Yup. I know. It's time to go. Let's go because it's time to go, Katherine."

It should have been plain to anyone watching or reading this at home that I was drunk. Beyond drunk. Like, one-more-sip-and-I-was-going-to-throw-up-from-alcohol-poisoning kind of drunk. The intoxication certainly numbed the confusion, but I still had to get out of there.

With Katherine.

But we just stood there.

Together.

Holding each other.

And I wondered how long this could last. Could I just stay here forever? Her scent was more intoxicating than the alcohol, a vanilla lotion of some sort or another. The skin of her neck was soft against my face. The weight of her arms wrapped around me was almost as comforting as her breast pressed up against mine.

Perhaps she didn't realize it, but it was exactly the tonic I needed after the betrayal I'd felt she'd perpetrated.

Maybe it was stupid to think so.

Maybe I was just drunk.

I don't know how long we stood there together like that, and I'm not exactly sure what prompted us to move on, but I remember her getting my arm around her neck and the two of us walking out of the bar together.

I remember, as we passed through the threshold of the front door, looking over to the storage closet where Katherine had disappeared. Standing, darkened in the doorway, was the Colonel. A smile on his face and a friendly hand raised as if to say goodbye to me and to thank me for Katherine.

The alcohol in my system was the only thing that made me not want to throw up from that last gesture. I knew it wouldn't make me feel any better or worse than I felt already.

Unless I could throw up on *him*.

Katherine and I walked arm in arm to my office, never saying a word. What could I have said? I didn't want to seem so accusatory. And I wasn't even sure if I should've been hurt by what she'd done. I didn't own her. I had no right to be upset, or at least that's what I told myself.

I fumbled with the keys when we arrived but managed to find the right one and insert it into the slot of the lock. I twisted the knob, the door opened, and I flipped on the lights.

The pair of us went straight for the futon.

As much as I was disappointed with what happened, I still wanted to just cuddle with her.

Was that so much to ask?

I collapsed down onto the futon, and she did the same but with the space of a person between us.

Not being able to bring myself to talk, I stood and went over to the record player. Resisting the urge to play Sinatra's version of "The Lady is a Tramp," I put on the B-side of Henry Mancini's Pink Panther soundtrack. Aside from the circus music at the end, I'd found that it was the perfect bit of decorative music for a romantic mood.

And that's how I felt: betrayed but romantic. I was aware of the cognitive dissonance in that feeling, but the alcohol helped reconcile the odd dichotomy.

I still couldn't think of anything to say to her, though.

Mancini's music began with a pop and a hiss, and I made my way back to the futon. I plopped down right where I was before and raised my hand up, resting it on the top edge of the couch.

I had no need to beckon her to come closer; she did that of her own volition. She still hadn't said much, so I still wasn't sure how to feel about anything, but I would give her the benefit of the doubt.

Nestling her head into the crook between my arm and chest, she placed a hand on my stomach. The smell of her hair, her shampoo mixed with the smoky beer smell of the bar, was a revelation to me. It came together in my nose as a mango sort of alcohol with that hint of vanilla from her lotion, and that scent would forever signal to me what was, what should be, and what could've been. And, perhaps, what still could be.

She nuzzled her face into my chest and tightened her grip on my stomach. I reached down and put my hand around her shoulder, holding her just as tenderly as she held me.

And then, after a moment like that, two small words came quietly from her. "I'm sorry."

Those words sent a shiver down my back the same way her breath on my neck had.

Sitting there, holding her in the dim light to the soft, slow piano and brass tones of Mancini's "Royal Blue," I wondered what would happen in the future.

Would we cross the Colonel's shows off our list of things we did together? Would we say goodnight later that evening and really mean goodbye? Would I go mad from frustrated jealousy and turn into a hulking monster she never wanted to see again?

I had no idea.

After suppressing the urge to want to punch the Colonel in the face, I wished I could just speak with him. He was so good with words and lyrics, I wondered what he would've said about the situation had he known exactly what was going on.

And then I realized that you don't talk to the Colonel.

You listen to him.

Because he was a poet warrior in the classic sense.

I could deal with the aftermath, the horror, another day. But in that moment, I'd take in Katherine's smell, the touch of her against me, the dizziness of the booze, and the feelings stirred by the music, and I'd figure it all out some other time.

Perhaps she was so drunk anyway that I'd have to remind her of what happened the same way I'd had to remind that I'd told her I loved her.

Oh well.

C'est la vie.

ROSY
DENIS FEEHAN

I made dinner tonight—
Irish stew, Irish whiskey.
I bought her that ring,
though the bank may arrest me.

But that circle of gold
with ornate filigree
came with a price:
my mounting agony.

See, Rosy had managed
to penetrate my heart
like Cupid's true arrow,
Leonardo's sweet art.

I offered the ring,
my stomach was tightening,
then I savored the glow
of love's lovely lightening.

I popped the champagne
and poured some for Rosy,
slid onto the couch,
getting close, getting cozy.

We laughed, and we kissed,
and we planned out our life,
but all I was thinking
she's to be my wife!

THE WEEPING WILLOW AT GOBLIN CREEK

MCKEL JENSEN

WE WERE the girls who looked alike. Our peers and teachers constantly asked if we were sisters, but as far as we knew, we had no relation, no common thread on a family tree unless you count our weeping willow as family—which we could both claim.

"We're fourth cousins on my mother's side," I would lie when people asked, but the truth was, we had no idea what a fourth cousin was.

We met one afternoon after school when I decided to take a long way home in the hopes of avoiding my sister's annoying friends. I stumbled upon a beautiful tree off the path behind my neighborhood. Laurel was already sitting under it, reading a book. She had long, thick, brown hair with her bangs braided to the side. Having just moved here with her family from California, she'd been out exploring and discovered this place as a perfect reading haven.

"Hey," I said. "What an amazing hideout! Can I join you?"

"Sure, come sit down," she responded. "My name is Laurel. Would you like a Fruit Roll-Up? I have an extra." Laurel reached inside a small backpack and handed me a treat.

And that was that. We were instant friends—as if we'd known each other for years.

Our willow tree, just barely out of view of suburban fences and sodded lawns, became our sanctuary. Sometimes, we could hear a nearby street, and every Friday was interrupted by the buzz of a distant lawnmower, but there in that field was our wilderness—our suburban oasis.

Laurel used to laugh at the way I said things. "Why do you say 'spirit-chul' instead of 'spiritual'?" she asked.

"I don't know," I responded. "That is just how I talk—that's how everyone talks," I said, still wondering what was so weird about it.

Soon after, she asked me to say "spiritual mountain" and laughed even harder when it came out as "spirit-chul mow-un."

I will admit it was funny to see how much she enjoyed this joke. She also helped me realize that our school's name, Cottonwood, did in fact have two *t*'s in it.

From the beginning, we loved to find adventure. Behind my neighborhood ran a creek. Whenever we didn't have school, we would cut through the parking lot at the Presbyterian Church on Vine Street and climb the levee to the grassy path along the waterway we called "Goblin Creek."

"Do you think the goblins have been there?" Laurel asked.

"What are we? Five?" I retorted, but in my heart, I believed the goblins had done their magic yet again in bringing our place to life. "I hope we'll see their magic," I resigned.

"Maybe we should start calling them hobgoblins," Laurel said, "I learned in Ms. Baker's Shakespeare class that goblins are the mean ones, but hobgoblins are magical."

"Right," I said, pretending to have heard the term *hobgoblin* before. "But then we'd have to change the name of our place to Hobgoblin Creek." The thought of this made my stomach hurt.

"Nah. Let's keep it Goblin Creek. It's our place. I don't think they would mind. Plus, I brought them gifts." In Laurel's palm were six or seven coins of various sizes. "Look at these. I'm sure they'll bring us luck."

"Where did you get those?" I asked.

We stood there out of view from the main street inspecting each one of them. I recognized the letters enough to know some were from Mexico, and I believe one said Finland, but the others had characters I'd never seen before.

"These are amazing," I said, holding each one to inspect their weight, size, and value.

"Thanks," Laurel said, "My dad had some old coins he let me have. I think he got them from the days when he traveled a lot."

"Does he not travel anymore?"

"No. Not anymore," she said. "He got a job here and wants to stay. Mom and I love having him around more often."

Our feet sunk into the earth, damp from the morning dew.

"Come on," I said. "Let's get to the hideout."

From there, we traveled further up the creek, behind many unsuspecting backyards, until the path opened up to a field.

The hobgoblins had performed their magic: the willow tree stood a hardy stone's throw from the creek in an opening of wild grass. Its branches touched the ground like my arms did when I laid on my belly on my bed, my fingers gently playing with the carpet fibers at the beginning of the day.

The young leaves of grass tenderly stretched from the earth, unaware of anyone watching, yet enjoying its newfound freedom from the dormant ground. The leaves of the willow tree barely emerged and had not quite showed off their true full-leaf glory, but it was clear—magical creatures had been here.

Laurel and I ran to the tree, inspecting the ground around it before parting the budding curtains to enter. Inside, Laurel placed her mat on a dry patch to sit and pulled out her coins. After inspecting each once again, I stood up and marched five paces north, then two paces east—making sure to compensate for any length of stride gained from my winter growth spurt. I knelt down, opened my backpack that was half full of snacks and notebooks for the day, and pulled out a small hand shovel. I dug down in that exact spot to reveal a metal box.

"You found it!" Laurel exclaimed.

I walked back over to the trunk, where Laurel was already halfway through with her Coke. The second I sat down next to her, we had the box open.

"Oh my goodness," she exclaimed, pulling out a BeBop magazine from two years before. We'd wrapped it in plastic to preserve it, yet some of the edges looked damp. "I can't believe I liked Jonathan. He looks so weird in this picture."

"What are you talking about? I remember you wanted to marry him." I said.

"That's not true." She began to defend herself before finding the plastic, machine-bought rings we bought on our way home from a movie.

"Remember," she asked laughing, "remember when we got these and that lady thought they were real?"

"She thought we stole them," I exclaimed. "She couldn't believe we were old enough to own something so nice."

"Little did she know," Laurel smiled.

We laughed at the contents of the box for as long as there was stuff to gawk over before putting our new treasures inside: six various sized coins from around the world.

"Do you think the goblins will take them?" I asked, forgetting our conversation about calling them hobgoblins.

"Why wouldn't they?" she asked. "But I don't think they'll take them soon. Look at the creek." Laurel pointed to the creek, and it was clear the water was too high, and the hobgoblins would be too busy this time of year to collect their gifts.

Through most of the late spring and into summer, the creek had slow-moving water. When the water was shallower than it was at that time, the water appeared to be green. The two of us loved to imagine a world of enchantment living under the creek, making the waters that color. We could never see what they were doing, but we liked to think they were always watching.

"What do you think the hobgoblins do all winter?" I asked. "Do you think they hibernate, or do they travel somewhere warm to live?"

"I think they're always down there," Laurel said, throwing a rock and watching it splash in the fast current. "They like to keep things in order."

As the spring turned into summer, the willow tree's curtains brought us shelter from the sun. I would bring my radio and an extra set of D batteries so we could listen to the latest pop songs. Laurel would bring a new Tiger Beat magazine, and we would dream about Freddie Prince Jr., Justin Timberlake, or Christian Bale, all the while drinking our soda through Red Vine licorice straws. Mainly, I would dream about my movie star career and my handsome celebrity husband, and Laurel would daydream of making films that would change the world.

This was our favorite way to spend our summer. Who knows where those dreams disappeared to. Perhaps I decided there was more to life than just the dream of twinkling lights of Hollywood, but I believe her dream was for real. I always believed they were real. I knew she would have changed the world if only she could have lived a little while longer.

I didn't realize what that place meant to me until Laurel stopped coming as often. It was the summer before our eighth-grade year. Sometimes I went alone to Goblin Creek, but if she couldn't come, I preferred to lock myself in the cool basement and watch a rented video. I got really frustrated with her when she would tell me she couldn't come.

"My mom won't let me come today," she told me over the phone.

I wrapped that telephone coil around my finger so many times the tip of my finger would turn purple. "What do you mean? You haven't been able to come all week," I said.

It was silent on the other end. Finally, she whispered, "I know."

I couldn't imagine what I was doing so wrong to make her not want to come hang out with me. Did her parents think I was a bad influence? Did she have other friends, another life, a boyfriend she wasn't telling me about?

She told me she had to go, and that was it. That was all I heard from her that week.

The following week, we met at my house and walked out of the neighborhood, up Vine Street, through the Presbyterian church's parking lot. The awkwardness was thick. Each step was calculated, and each word was met with a sideways glance. I didn't want to do or say anything that would take my best friend away. Until we reached the willow.

"I have an extra bag of Cheese Puffs if you want it," I said, trying to be as natural as possible but falling short.

Laurel gazed through the canopy to the creek. She waned a smile and said, "No, thank you."

"I brought water too," I said in a desperate attempt to give her something that would make things normal again. Perhaps she liked healthier choices now; I didn't know.

She shook her head.

I tried one last time to offer her something before she interrupted.

"I have cancer," she said. "My cancer is out of remission."

I stood there. I'd heard grownups talk about cancer before, but Laurel wasn't a grown up. I also knew she was sick before arriving in Utah, but I didn't realize—

"So, it wasn't something I did?" I asked, feeling my lungs expand with new air.

"Did? You didn't give me cancer." Laurel shook her head confused.

"No—" My voice stuck in my throat. "No, I mean—you're not mad at me?"

Laurel displayed a wry smile and then settled in, curling over her legs with a sigh.

"I thought that was why you were avoiding me," I said.

"No. Never. No way." And then she was back. "No, I've had a lot of tests done this week. I couldn't say anything until we were sure."

At the time, I had no way to comprehend what all she had to do. Laurel taught me what leukemia did to the body and how radiation worked. I had no idea what *chemo* did or what the phrase "out of remission" actually entailed. I didn't know that each time a person's cancer came back, it was harder to fight.

When school started, Laurel didn't return. Her parents were concerned about her getting sick from the kids there, but they would let her come over still. On the days that we could, we would sneak back to our willowy sanctuary, but many days she just asked to watch a movie at the house, and then my dad would drive her home.

Soon, she didn't come to my house at all, and I spent some afternoons during the week with her in her room since she didn't feel like doing much. But we yearned to go back to Goblin Creek—to our willow, to feel our feet in the dirt. We wanted to see what our magical friends had done while we'd been away. What colors did they put on display?

Laurel became gaunt; her hair thinned until her parents threw a party and shaved it. I considered shaving my head too, but I didn't. I'm not really sure why. It was confusing how happy everyone was when my friend was dying. People brought her gifts, and her house was always decorated like it was her birthday with balloons and banners. Even my parents took me out to dinner more often and let me choose where we ate. It was like everyone was pretending nothing bad was going on—or perhaps overcompensating. I just wanted people to act normal.

Winter came, and I imagined how the tree looked in the snow. Sometimes a winter storm in Utah would give us three feet of snow that would cancel school and give us a snow day to play outside, but that year, whatever trace of snow that fell didn't last long. Laurel was really sick, so she couldn't go out much anyway. I ventured out to the willow tree every couple of weeks just to check on things. That winter, I found the ground barren and hard. The creek had all but dried up, and the branches of our willow tree had nothing to give; it gave no shelter, and its lifeless limbs whipped in the wind instead of gliding with it. What kind of trick were these hobgoblins playing? Why did they take so much away in such a short time? The ground beneath it was too frozen to even draw my name in the dirt.

Cold and rejected, I went home.

When I arrived home, my mom sat down on the couch next to me. I had been trying to eat some mini pizzas, but they had already gone cold. I wasn't hungry anyway.

"Hi, darling. How are you doing?" she asked, putting her hand on my knee.

"Fine." I responded, having started my training in the arts of teenage/parent conversations. It didn't divert her, though.

"I heard from Laurel's mom today," she said.

My silence let her know I was listening.

"Her medication isn't working," she said.

I didn't respond. I didn't know what to think. In my head, I was screaming at her to stop talking—to not finish what she was saying, but I couldn't get any sound.

Mom paused, then said, "Laurel's medication isn't working. The doctors don't know why, and they don't know what else to do."

All I wanted was to run back to our tree, to go back to how things were, to laugh and dream again with my friend. But I sat there on my couch, with my mother's arms wrapped around me, weeping.

That was it, then. The leukemia wasn't giving up.

Three months later, on April 6, 1994, Laurel passed away in her home.

The day she died, I walked to Goblin Creek. I left our neighborhood, crossed the back parking lot of the Presbyterian Church, climbed the levee, and walked to our place. The ground was muddy and hard to walk in. Our weeping willow looked bare and dismal, and there was no sign of the hobgoblins anywhere. The whole year I'd held it together, but when I made it to the willow, I fell to my knees in tears of loss, anguish, and loneliness. I was covered in mud and didn't care.

I cried. I knew she was free of the disease that took her. Yet, I was angry at having such little time with her. We were fourth cousins after all; shouldn't that count for something? Also, why take her away and not me. I wasn't the one with a plan; I was the one who didn't know what she was doing. "I'm not even that good in school!" I exclaimed.

To this day, I don't know who I was talking to. The willow? Some hidden magical creatures? God? I didn't care.

I reached into my backpack for my little shovel, paced five steps north, two steps east, and began to dig. I used the shovel for a short time before I abandoned it for my hands, and I dug until I got the box. The mud made the box slippery and harder to open, but when it did, I grabbed the coins. By the time I was able to look at them, they were unreadable from the muck I'd put on them by handling them with dirty hands. Dark clouds moved in, and the sky turned black as if the day had never come. I stayed there at Goblin Creek for several hours holding those coins in my hand. I was there by myself, but I didn't feel alone. I felt the eyes of our magical friends watching me, and I imagined that Laurel was there too.

When I was ready, I stood up, walked over to the shallow creek, and threw every coin in there—value be damned!

"Take 'em!" I screamed. "Take every. Last. One of them." When the last one disappeared beneath the green water, I let out a yell that had been building up for months. When I saw a back porchlight turn on from behind one of those suburban fences, I knew it was time to go.

The next few days were dreary. The dark clouds wept down on all of us without letting up much. It wasn't until the day of her funeral that the sky cleared. I've never seen a sky so clear and blue as I did that day.

Just hours before her funeral, I managed to make it back to Goblin Creek. The hobgoblins had been busy. There were flowers, yellow and white, on the ground that I'd never seen there before in years past, and the wild grass was alive. I know that the official first day of spring is the third week of March, but after seeing the creek that day, I declared that day its real first day. Piled at the base of our willow tree were six neatly stacked coins.

I wept silently as I watched Laurel's casket be placed into the ground and as the family shoveled the dark dirt on top. Laurel was buried in Dawn Cemetery directly underneath a budding willow tree. It was the first time in days that the dark blanket of clouds didn't keep close watch over me and our town. It was the first time in days I was able to see the sky clearly.

HERE FOR PICKUP

HEIDI VOSS

I'VE BEEN WORKING for centuries as a conductor between the temporal world of Earth and the Garden of Truth, and so far I've never dealt with a human soul who could refuse my summon to the next life. That is, until I reached for Martin Navarro's hand.

Most people I deal with know death is coming. They've been seriously ill or injured, or they've reached the later years of their life and are finished watching the earth rotate around the sun. Each morning, I press my hands together in prayer and ask, "Who needs guidance today?" When I open my hands, I see a name. Yesterday, my traveler was Praskovya Kozlov, and I met her in a hospital in Krasnodar Krai to bring her from a life of joint pain and movie reruns to fields of blossoms that can be eaten to gain celestial knowledge.

Younger travelers tend to object the most when I arrive. They yell that they haven't fulfilled their purpose, as if life were an enormous manufacturing line and they mustn't be released until they've assembled a certain number of metaphorical car mufflers. When they're done throwing pots and pans at me or crying until they grow sleepy, I take their hand and ease the spirit from their body. Their chest fills with warmth, their fears fade, and I tell them about the many luscious delicacies made from blossoms the angels have prepared for them.

When I meet Martin Navarro, I step through the wall of his home and stand before him. "I'm here for pickup."

He looks up from his recliner, wearing a white shirt and brown slacks peppered with black cat fur. "Are you from the sandwich shop? You know me too well. I haven't even placed my order yet." He eases out of his chair and shuffles to the kitchen, digging through his wallet for bills.

I follow him to the kitchen, increasing the brightness of my heavenly glow. Some travelers don't recognize me as a divine being right away, and I hate to shock them by taking their hand too soon. "Martin, it's your time. You've completed your Earthly journey."

He smiles and pockets his wallet. "Oh, you're an angel, are you? Come to take me to my final reward or punishment?"

I exhale, keeping my countenance calm and serene but internally wishing humans would stop perpetuating unsophisticated notions that good behavior equals halos and clouds and bad behavior equals horns and lava. I reach out my hand and use my go-to phrase: "You have a life of beauty and transcendence waiting for you. Take my hand, and we'll go together."

He shakes his head, brow contracting. "You seem very nice, miss, but no, I won't be going with you today."

I draw my hands together, praying for strength. Lately, my travelers all seem too attached to this mortal plane. "I know this next step may seem daunting, but I assure you it includes a release from earthly worries, pain, and heartache. Instead of limping to one side, you could run and leap."

Martin's hand reaches for his left leg, and he presses his

lips together. "Miss, that sounds tempting, but I have someone who relies on me here. I won't be leaving this old, creaky body just yet."

I rub my forehead and wonder if humanity would reach self-actualization as a whole much quicker if each individual didn't have to be coerced into ascension. I'd like to make other pickups today rather than squabbling with one old man.

I reach for his hand anyway, prepared to take his soul with me whether he likes it or not. I grasp the cool feel of his consciousness for a moment, the citrus fragrance of his essence filling my nose . . . then it's gone. His hand slips from mine. I try again and can't seem to get a good grip.

I grit my teeth. "Stop this foolishness, Martin."

"You're welcome to stay for lunch if you like. I can start a pot of ravioli." He opens the fridge and holds up a package of pasta with a picture of Italy on the side.

I stride toward the wall. "Enjoy your lunch."

Outside, I examine Martin's home. He doesn't appear to have any special sigils in his yard or spells placed to impede my work. Given the appearance of his home, I wouldn't guess he's trained in any dark art that would allow him to slip through the grasp of death. Why, then, can I not hold on to his spirit?

Perhaps another conductor will be able to escort Martin to the next life. I press my palms together and repeat my prayer. "Who needs guidance today?" The name Paulo Valle stretches across my hands. I walk through the sky, the way parting before me, and hope Paulo doesn't give me the same trouble Martin has.

I guide more souls to the Garden of Truth. The earth rotates. I pray for my next traveler, and Martin Navarro appears on my hands once more. I walk toward his home, hoping this will be a different Martin Navarro.

"Are you Mrs. Park's girl? I thought you were coming tomorrow to work on the lawn." Martin dumps a tin of cat food into a bowl in the kitchen.

I clear my throat. "I'm here for pickup. Martin, you've had one day more to say your goodbyes. Please take my hand."

Martin frowns and, again, shakes his head. "I'm sorry, but I can't come today either."

I tilt my head to one side. "You can't come, huh? Someone relies on you?" I wonder if he has a favorite grandchild he dotes on or a church fundraiser he helps with. "Even if you serve needs here, others will step in when you're gone. Life goes on when you pass."

He pulls a plastic container from above the microwave and opens the lid. "Do you want a muffin while you're here? My daughter brought them by."

I take a seat at the counter, studying him. "Is she the person you feel you need to stay for? I'm sure she's perfectly able to care for herself."

He pushes the container closer to me.

I reach for his hand again, catching the cool touch of his spirit, but again he slides through my grip.

"Do you want banana nut or blueberry?" He tilts the container toward me so I can see rows of squished muffins.

I stand and head for the nearest wall. "I don't eat, Martin."

The next two times I visit Martin, I surprise him. Instead of announcing my presence, I reach through his chair to try and snatch his soul. He must feel it because his attention is drawn, and he hurries to the kitchen to offer me something.

I sweep through his house, looking for hidden stashes of

magic or spiritual knowledge. I check through photo albums, looking for trips overseas where he may have learned a mental trick for making his spirit slippery. When he sees me flipping through his photos, he sits in the chair next to me and tells me about his college days on the swimming and diving team and the failed bike repair company he tried out in his garage.

"I never could get the hang of tuning gears on the fancy new bikes with all kinds of attachments and cords and doohickeys." He waves a hand. "Besides, I like riding bikes more than I like fixing them."

I close the album and return it to the shelf. "You can ride a bike again if you come with me, Martin."

He leans back in his chair and closes his eyes. "That sounds like a wonderful time, my dear, but I'm not coming with you today."

The next day, I sit with Martin in his living room, watching a movie on television. He's set out a sandwich and glass of milk for me, though I've explained my physical form has no need for food and can't process it.

I rest my head on my chin. "I'm impressed how the characters in this film look so chipper while dancing such challenging choreography."

The ice cubes in Martin's glass clink as he takes a sip of orange juice. "That's how it used to be in these movies. Their feet move a million miles an hour, and you wouldn't know it from the smiles on their faces."

My eyes narrow. "The actors from this movie have all passed, you know. If you come with me, you can meet them."

His eyebrows raise. "Wouldn't that be something, to sit down with one of these fellas and ask what it was like to make history?"

I lean over the arm of the couch. "You know what I'm here for, Martin. Take my hand."

He stands and limps to the kitchen. "I'm sorry, miss. See you tomorrow."

The next time I visit Martin, I help him with a jigsaw puzzle featuring an illustration of a café. I explain to him that life isn't a puzzle to solve and that he doesn't need to find an answer before he passes. He brings me another cup of warm tea, replacing the untouched cup he placed before me earlier.

The day after, he reads me a chapter of his favorite book, *Oliver Twist*. I tell him he can read many books at once by dining on the food of the angels, but he assures me Dickens is best enjoyed one page at a time.

The next day, Martin seems upset, and asks me to sit in the garden while he takes care of something inside. I've seen every inch of his house and can't imagine what he must do while I'm away, but I sit on a swing on the back porch and gaze at the small variety of plant life available in this biome of earth, considering how I might convince him to travel with me. What if he never leaves his home and causes some kind of logical paradox that messes with the flow of time and space? I hope I won't get in trouble for it. I've been a quality conductor for many years.

He slides open the glass door. "Can I get you anything, miss?"

I shake my head. "You look pale today, Martin."

His chin trembles, and he takes a seat next to me. "Nothing a bit of bird watching won't help."

"Sparrows grow in abundance here, don't they?" I kick my

feet back and forth as I watch a flock of them peck at a feeder on a pole in the yard. I know a great many iridescent bird varieties in the Garden of Truth, but a tight feeling in my gut warns me to keep quiet about the journey today.

Martin points to a block of suet in a cage near the feeder. "If we're lucky, we might see a woodpecker today. I saw one out the window last week while I was washing dishes. He must have been male since he had a bright red patch on the back of his head."

"What a delight to see a woodpecker." Sure, a woodpecker may be a somewhat dull Earth bird, but if we see one, Martin might be cheered a bit. I hope one passes through.

The next day, my stomach lurches at the sight of another conductor outside Martin's house. Have I been deemed unfit to assist him on his journey?

"Ah, good to see a fellow every now and then. Peaceful travels, Sondeil." The other conductor greets me with shining, blue eyes and a mop of thick, straight hair.

His name forms in my mind, and I give him a short bow. "Peaceful travels, Gavreel." I step closer and see a black cat curled up in his arms. My shoulders loosen. He isn't here for Martin. "You've been assigned animal spirits?"

Gavreel gazes down at the cat and strokes his head. "I'm grateful to be in such a blessed role. These creatures can still be a handful, but they're often a bit more cooperative than humans."

I run a hand through my hair. "Tell me about it." As my gaze roves over the black fur of the cat in Gavreel's arms, a flash bursts in my mind, popping like fireworks. I give another quick bow to the conductor and walk past him.

I jog to the front door and pause. Instead of stepping through, I rap on the door. "I'm here for pickup," I call softly.

The home is quiet. It's usually quiet, but the air was always bright with the bustle of Martin fixing something in the kitchen or peacefully serene with the reverberations of his spirit dreaming in the recliner.

The door creaks open, and Martin stands before me in a charcoal gray suit, baggy around the shoulders. He carries a suitcase in one hand and a hat in the other.

I exhale a breath, my mouth tugging into a smile. "You won't need all that."

He sets down his suitcase and passes his hat from hand to hand. "I wasn't sure how else to prepare."

I wrinkle my forehead. "The last few days must have been difficult for you."

Martin wipes his eyes with a handkerchief. "I'm sure they've been just as difficult for you."

"I don't often get to know people much on the job, so it was a nice change of pace." I shrug.

Martin pulls his hat onto his head.

I hold out my hand.

LEAP OF FAITH

MARIE TOLLSTRUP

THE WRITING ACT, not unlike skydiving, involves fear and freedom. Just before that leap into empty space, one not only resists but also dreads vaulting from the plane, but once one is in flight, the views stun to the point of exhilaration. Once I began writing, I was spiritually moved, and as I progressed, plumbing the depths of my soul's psyche, my spirit expanded, extending to everyone in my orbit. I started with faith—faith to believe my inklings were worth recording. Words, when juxtaposed just right, create magic and, in some cases, sacred worlds.

Despite having taught writing for over forty years, I rarely found either the time or inclination to write, except for fledgling poetry when I was single. A gem line comes to mind: "Tree your love to me." Stephen Dunning, the poet, had inspired me at an Ojai Writing Conference. But toying with words had not been part of the daily sustenance nurturing my being.

Ross Shickler, my co-principal, stood framed in my classroom doorway. I invited him in. He leaned over the *Stylus* layout page I was critiquing. "So . . . what will you do when you retire?" he posed, a smile playing on his lips.

"Rest and relax!" I blurted. "Haven't given it a thought."

"You should write," Ross said. "Take up the pen as you ask your students to do." He had cast a seed.

He was rewriting his own book on Canadian trout fishing. His new publisher wanted more detail. When Ross sought my advice for fleshing out his text, I opened my Creative Writing files to him. Derrydale Press published his book, *Lake Trout: North America's Greatest Game Fish*, in 2001.

Having just moved from California, my husband Burke and I were corralled by boxes. The stifling mid-July heat was oppressive. Besides unpacking and putting our new home in order, I prayed and meditated. How would I survive in this strange land? I floated in misery without purpose, uprooted from family, friends, an established home, work, and a familiar environment. The first anchor in my exile was composing a syllabus to guide adults to write their life stories. If my high school students could write impressive, award-winning tales of their truncated lives, I believed adults could write compelling stories of their extended life adventures. I set goals. By December, the syllabus for Writing Your Memoir existed, and by spring, I launched my course at Dixie State College's Community Education program. I was never disappointed.

How wonderful that life does not go according to best-laid projections. An unexpected path revealed itself. Committed to guiding adults in exploring their life stories, I commenced my own story. I also wanted to answer my own gnawing question that devoured my confidence: could I write? Adults would not be as forgiving as teens if I did not model what I challenged them to do. How does one launch a memoir? I used the eternal advice—*in media res*—to leap into the middle of things.

I grounded my first chapter by describing the setting of my

roots, a northern Wisconsin potato farm where I returned to visit my parents. Walking a familiar gravel road past the ruins of my first childhood home, I flashed back to dreaded violent scenes I had witnessed as a child. A pattern of survival emerged. I chanced upon the beginning of my writing journey.

As I composed, I stumbled upon writing strategies I could share with my adults. How do you overcome writer's block? Stare the blank-paged tiger in the eye, and claim your trophy. Click away at the keyboard. Delete what you don't like. Try again. Stories that were buried deep inside me caught fire, consuming entire pages. Narratives took on life and meandered from page to page. I began to make sense of my life in the framework of the stories I was compelled to tell. They stirred me, motivating me to continue recording my life odyssey. I became my own therapist, decoding what had happened to me. A new existence I had once dreaded lay open before me where I discovered spiritual insights.

My stories became my companions as did other tasks throughout the day. No longer did I feel empty when I settled before my computer. My synapses sparked. I jotted down the flow of ideas on notepads. Only if I were midstream in a story did these flagstone ideas present themselves. New elements found their way into my stories: essential dialogue, body language, opposing characters, transcendent insights. I welcomed feeling productive, expanding awareness of how I had become me. Exploring my childhood offered a rich tapestry of incidents. I was blessed, becoming addicted.

An irritating burr story had haunted me for years. At teacher conferences, a presenter would ask attendees to write about a childhood incident. Like a reoccurring overture, I returned to Karen's premature death. My stack of vignettes grew. She had fallen off a table at three and one-half months and died two weeks later. This first encounter with death when I had just turned seven had never left my consciousness. This story's time had ripened. Details spilled forth. My feisty, red-headed sister had turned over and fallen with a thud to the floor while Mom turned to retrieve a diaper. Karen disappeared from our lives and reemerged in our living room as a cold, beautiful doll. The icy good-bye kiss, polishing my white shoes, crunching golden leaves, and Mom's grieving wails dominated the funeral day.

By recording this childhood trauma in detail, I experienced a spiritual catharsis, not unlike what the Greeks felt when they reenacted recent battle scenes on stage in their amphitheaters.

I felt drawn to a writers' support group. By February, I amassed courage to attend a meeting and learned they were publishing a twenty-fifth-anniversary anthology. I submitted a honed copy of my Karen story, which was published in their anthology. By June, members were entering the statewide League of Utah Writers' annual writing contest. Following my advice to my students, *You can't win if you don't enter*, I dared to submit *Karen's Bridge*. Summer transformed to fall. While opening my email, I read Marissa's message: "Have you heard the news? You've won first place in the Inspirational Personal Experience category."

My heartbeat quickened. I wept freely, tears blurring the trees outside my front window. This was a private, sacred moment. I knew I had a gift to teach writing, confirmed by my students' awards and publications, but now I perceived I was an anointed writer, one whose words could move readers. Indeed, I could write.

My family grew up with secrets, secrets no one dared unearth. My siblings and I witnessed Dad's drunken bouts when he accosted Mom at night, leaving behind the brutality of domestic violence. The pall of darkness reminded us to keep this knowledge covert. Chronic yelling matches solved anyone's hearing problem in our household. Years later while Dad was institutionalized, I learned he was analyzed as a paranoid schizophrenic.

How does one break this code of silence? Even if I were tempted to omit or gloss over these embarrassing family ghosts, the reader would know I had left out some life-shaping forces. One never slips through life without the branding of searing pain.

Once these private details were revealed in print, I felt guilty because Dad also possessed an impassioned, generous nature. I felt compelled to record his worthy work ethic which made him a successful businessman, expanding his kingdom from a fledgling farm of eighty acres to over seven hundred. Not until I narrated incidents where Dad revered his land, financed a Piper Cub flight to view the family farm, and provided a home to a World-War-II-displaced Polish family did I reveal Dad's balanced portrait. Not only was I seeking fairness but I was also seeking to forgive Dad for his grave sins. I discovered compassion for my flawed father, a soulful cathartic moment.

Mom acted as a harbor to her eight children, but I never fully appreciated the impact of her stable love. Through story after layered story, she emerged, like a hidden Polaroid as a larger-than-life figure, a strong beacon. Mom instilled her stalwart faith in her children, inspiring us to go forth and live with honor. She had an instinct for raising children, a dash of adventurous flair mixed with staunch sanity. My stories stand as an immortal legacy to my mother's saintly heroism.

Writing is a powerful channel for understanding our mutual tragedies and provides healing as we cope with life's toughest battles. Through letters my husband and I composed to our bipolar son, Thad, while he was in prison, we made sense out of his and our world. Through recording phases of

my husband's four surgeries battling melanoma and squa-
mous cancers, I was able to sustain myself through nursing
him for 5.5 years. When I chanced upon Flash Fiction, where a
story is distilled in less than one thousand words, I was
hooked by this challenge. I found it the perfect vehicle to
capture the titillation of my post-Convent first date at Chica-
go's Playboy Club, the thrill of the first guy who fell for me,
and the horror of a date rape.

While attending a writing workshop, I learned a foolproof
way to pen a poem: choose an extended metaphor that carries
the message. I compared vulnerable workshop attendees to
knights wearing armor who come to consult with Arthur
around his table, carrying their quiver of words like arrows in
my winning *Workshop* poem. Only when I joined a poetry
critique group did both my poetic productivity and prowess
improve. Poetry comforted me when my husband died of
metastatic melanoma, and I joined a grieving group. Instead of
journaling my grieving progression after each session, I chose
poetry to document my universal journey of loss, which I
shared with my fellow mourners the next session. Poetry
became my philosophical conch through which I could speak
my emotional truth. Poetry proved to be the grace I needed to
survive without my beloved.

Once I decided to write, the process of my metamorphosis
began, which possessed a mystical dimension. I gained both
emotional and spiritual insights through story and poem,
reaching depths of awareness I had never fathomed before. I
identified with the Apostle John's words: "In the beginning
was the Word, and the Word was with God, and the Word was
God." Akin to God, I re-created myself through the narratives
and lyrics I wrote. Stephen Sondheim attests, "Art, in itself, is
an attempt to bring order out of chaos." Like Sondheim, I
discovered my own stories and songs never materialized out

of order but appeared out of chaos because writing proved to be a messy process. Something that never existed before emerged, possessing immortality. While writing I gained a new footing, not unlike observing myself in an out-of-body experience. Writing gave me the chance to meet a transformed self, a transcendent self who is blessed every day I write. I don't regret taking that leap of faith that liberated me to be a ceaselessly evolving writer.

LAST NIGHT

GREG R. GOODMAN

I awaken with a headache.
The pounding is incessant.
Each heartbeat accentuates my agony.
If I knew state secrets, I would surely reveal them
for even a single aspirin.
Memories of last night slowly penetrate the heavy,
stew-like fog encasing my head, now starting to lift.
The mental residue of lust's intoxication
when the evening's fire is stoked with alcohol.
My tongue is parched and thick
as if wrapped in its own cozy, foreign language.

Trying to remain focused, I peer around the room.
There is a glow from filigree rainbows which dance transiently
along the far wall-
dance transiently along the far wall—
the final resting place of morning sunlight
reflected off champagne bubbles
still rising in my glass, half full near the window.
Scattered around the room are

the remnants of the evening's progress
defined by various articles of clothing and overturned bottles.
Your body next to me, transcendent, but motionless.
A single gunshot required to arrest that beautiful form.
You were always unpredictable. . . .
The pounding at the door, now fully realized,
achieves new clarity.

DARLING BUDS OF MAY

TRACEY G. BOYLE

"I'LL SET the tea up on the patio. Such a pleasant day." Gemma smiles at her father-in-law. "Mia is anxious for her walk about the garden."

John looks down at his three-year-old granddaughter. "Mrs. Randolph brought a cake. There, on the sideboard."

"Of course. You go on now," Gemma says.

John takes Mia's small and delicate hand into his, feeling privileged for the visit. Gemma had begun to come for weekly visits on Sundays while Peter was playing golf. A few months ago, John had finally met his little granddaughter.

"I would like to know my father-in-law," Gemma had said when he opened the door that first time. This was after Gemma had seen him entering the cancer center, although it took three visits before she brought it up.

John and Mia walk across the bright green lawn. Mia skips along at John's side, stopping to touch the silken petals of tulips growing in the herbaceous border. The birds celebrate the gorgeous weather, singing as if in conversation.

"Hurry up. Hurry up," a robin calls.

At the bottom of winding terrace steps, Mia pets the head

of a cement pony statue. John looks up the steps and recalls a 1912 photo of Great-Grandmother sitting near newly built stone walls that were clean, sturdy, and uncluttered by the various vines or flowering plants that have split and crumbled these walls over the past one hundred plus years. Maintaining the property is a lot of work, and John worries what will become of it. He relies on garden club volunteers who exchange their hours for his annual tours to raise money for their club or associated charities.

"Come to me, me. Come to me, me," a goldfinch sings.

He takes Mia's hand as they slowly ascend steps that are lined on one side with flowering pots, being careful to avoid creeping thyme that has grown over certain spots. The view from the top terrace is one John indulges in every day, over-looking rose beds, farm buildings, and the Devonshire coun-tryside in the distance.

Next, they descend through a narrow path surrounded by a field carpeted with blooming bluebells. Here are a few of the hundred oak trees John's father established years ago. Buster, John's chocolate Labradoodle, meets them and trots ahead, his ears flapping. Buster knows the way and occasionally turns around to be sure he is being followed.

"Be sweet. Be sweet to me," the song thrush beckons.

They step through an area naturalized with bulbs that have finished their annual display. When they reach the fence bordering the property, Mia places her tiny hands onto a gate's wooden railing. "Baa baa," she mimics sheep in the distance. "Where are the little lambs?"

John holds her up in his arms. "See, there," he says, point-ing, and then notices Mary Randolph approaching them.

"Hello, John," Mary greets him as she props her walking stick against a fence post, then adjusts her gray curls behind her ears. "And here's a sweet one." She pats Mia's cheek.

Mia sticks a finger into her mouth and turns her face into John's chest shyly.

"Have you been feeling well, John?"

"Wonderful now."

"Dinner on Tuesday?" Mary asks. "Bob looks forward to the chess challenge."

"Yes, Tuesday. I'll be there. Thank you, Mary."

Mary takes up her stick to continue the walk around the perimeter of her property.

I can hear you. I can hear you.

John and Mia move away from the gate, resuming their walk. They scrape past a fuchsia-colored camellia bush that towers above John's six-foot frame. The gentle sound of water splashing beneath a bridge leads them to Mia's favorite spot, where a swing hangs from a huge tulip poplar that reigns over a garden room. John lifts Mia onto the swing, and, keeping his gnarled and mottled hands over her plump, soft ones, John gives her a gentle push, looking into the eyes of May.

May . . . his May . . .

Gone from his bed one freezing, snowy, morning. Nowhere in the house. Panicking, hurrying to search the large property, visioning May frozen on the ground or face up in the stream. He hears her laughter and finds her here, where she is swinging, barefoot, in only her white gown, lips bluing. He removes his coat, wraps her up, and carries her to the house.

Racing between the kettle in the kitchen and the fireplace, poking dry sticks into a fire, and rubbing May's feet, where he had propped her into a chair, covering her in blankets.

Her eyes recognizing . . .

"John. Oh John."

A moment of lucidity . . .

"Yes, I'm John, my darling May."
Touching her cheek . . .
"I'm so sorry—sorry for this."
"Never. Don't be."
The kettle whistling . . .
Her looking, far away . . .
"Peter, has he come by?"
Green eyes tearing up . . .
Anger wells up from my heart, to my head, and out to the ends of my fingers. Her brief moments of lucidness, wasted on grief. Stolen—by our son!
"Don't leave me, John."
"Never. You're my May."
A few happy moments . . .
Then May is gone again. I hold her two hands in my own for a time, then go to tend the kettle in the kitchen.
I'll see you soon. I'll see you soon.

John and Mia enter the apple orchard, walking through planted wildflowers, while Buster runs ahead, poking his nose into the edges of overgrown grasses, sniffing for rabbits maybe. Some of the apple trees are covered with white flowers, promising a good harvest, while other cultivars lag behind. *Like children*, John thinks.
Like Peter . . .
The row they had had . . .
About him not visiting . . .
"Why? She doesn't know me."
"She has periods when she remembers."
"Not when I'm there."
"She cries. She misses you."
"Don't guilt trip me!"

"Selfish," I yell. "You owe your mother the time!"

There were more arguments, denials, resentment—the wedge that split John and his son apart. They stood next to each other at the funeral and never spoke a word . . . five years now.

John moves his finger beneath his eye wiping away a tear. He sees the house looming before them. He and Mia have walked full circle now. The front of the old, three-story, Elizabethan manor is covered with blooms of yellow climbing roses. Buster precedes them through the open door, then through a long hallway that leads out to the patio where Gemma waits for them at a table.

Gravel crunches on the drive outside the brick wall. *Maybe a garden club volunteer taking advantage of the nice weather*, John thinks. He places Mia onto a chair while Gemma begins to pour the tea. The metal latch on the gate clangs. John freezes as he sees his son, Peter, dressed in a polo shirt and khaki golf pants, walking toward them. He grabs the back of a chair, his heart skipping beats. John is lightheaded. All stops; no birds chirping, no tea dribbling into china cups, no perfume from Zephirine Drouhin roses climbing the brick wall, no soft, ruffling of wind to carry scent.

Seeing John's reaction, and then Peter, Gemma puts the teapot down. Looking scattered, almost fearful, she says to John, "I didn't know," as if it were her fault somehow.

He can't take his eyes off of his son. The birds sing. Roses perfume the air.

"I couldn't be more pleased," he says. Then turning to look Gemma directly in the eyes, he repeats, "I couldn't be more pleased."

Then Peter is at the table, looking tall, healthy, with his green eyes and blond hair.

"Daddy's here!" Mia bounces in her chair.

"Father," Peter says, and warily reaches his hand out to shake John's hand.

Looking into May's eyes, John shakes Peter's hand. "Have a seat, son. You're just in time for tea." John smiles and pulls a chair out for Peter, then one for himself.

Gemma begins to pour tea again, and then cuts the cake. The clinking of silverware against china plates melds with birdsong.

"I want biscuits, Mummy, not cake," Mia insists. "Grandad, you want a biscuit too?"

John looks at his family around the table, then at the expanse of gardens and countryside surrounding the old home while the birds call out encouragingly.

Begin again. Begin again.

HOMEBOUND

GRACE DIANE JESSEN

A SUDDEN STROKE at age ninety left her in a hospital bed, stripped of dignity, mobility, and memory of her grown-up years. She struggled through three long months in a rehab facility before being moved to her living room at home. There, she can look at photos on the wall of grandchildren and the great-grands, even though she cannot remember their names.

In her mind, childhood days in the little town across the mountain are clear as a polished window. She remembers the schoolyard where she played hopscotch with friends, purple irises growing along the fence of a little house her family called home, a nine-patch quilt her grandma made, and long walks to the pasture to bring the cows home for milking on summer evenings.

Yet her husband's face, his touch, his voice have vanished, blown away like dry leaves in a stiff wind. She does not remember where he worked, the bib overalls he often wore, that he didn't care to dance, or the little things he said to make her smile. Every day, two women come to visit. They say they are her daughters, but she does not remember giving birth, braiding their hair, walking with them to the school bus, or attending their weddings. She tries to talk, ask questions, but the weak, raspy sounds are difficult to understand.

A faithful caregiver has become the most familiar one now. She comes early every morning, tends to her needs, helps her eat, provides kind companionship, closes the blinds when she wants privacy, then tucks her in before going home at night. Sometimes it is after ten o'clock before she slips away.

On many mornings, others come. A home health nurse helps move her legs, her arms. A cleaning lady dusts the shelves, vacuums the floor. A delivery woman brings hot lunch in a box at noon. Before pandemic time, grandchildren, neighbors, friends stopped by, but fear of bringing a virus now keeps them away.

She tries to be cheerful, but wonders sometimes why days, months, years have become a lengthening parade. She remembers the Fourth of July when she was young, watching the procession down Main Street. Marching bands and floats came first; the people riding horses were always last. She begins to dream about the man she can't remember and wishes for horses.

OUT OF TIME

KYLIE N. BIRCH

MUSIC from the cell phone speaker swells in the solemn silence of the night. Slow and weightless, the notes weave an instrumental symphony conveying comfort and peace. But I feel neither of those things as I try to get comfortable on one of the metal folding chairs in our cramped living room, drifting in and out of restless sleep, wondering when the end will come.

I've been in knots for weeks at the realization that the farm is no longer the extra income of a teenager or newlywed. Instead, it is the vital lifeblood of our entire family, one passed down over generations—now likely to either die with the farmer or at his daughter's ineptitude of stepping into his place.

My head lulls, and I jolt awake, noting once again that only minutes have passed on the thermostat's small clock. 1:55. 1:58. 2:02. The white digits haloed by blue backlight carve away at the last precious moments we have left. Mom cries, which I try to ignore because I need to be strong, yet I feel as if my entire world is dropping out from under me and hurling me into painful unknowns. Unknowns I hadn't planned on facing within the next twenty years, let alone at age twenty.

This can't be happening. This isn't real.

But it is. It's been our reality for nearly four years now, though I quickly realize that not even the darkest stains of my imagination prepared me for the emotional upheaval. Just days earlier, I'd frantically cracked and scrambled and seasoned and prayed over some damned eggs—*Please, God. Please let him be able to eat these*—only to be in silent tears when Dad wordlessly used the fork to push them around his plate. He was starving yet too sick to eat them, wasting away in a rental Hospice chair, his sunken skin and jutting bones made more prominent by his 6'6" frame. The one that used to lift me onto horses and tip me upside down to walk on the ceiling— something the kids I don't even have yet will never get a chance to do with their grandpa, which Dad will never be.

I should've had kids right away. Then I could've at least told them they knew him for a short time.

Aunt Vickie monitors the morphine patch and medication, then grasps the stick attached to a small, pink sponge, dipping it in water and bringing it to Dad's chapped, whisker-framed lips that we attempted to shave days earlier. No slurping. No swallowing. No surprise to anyone strewn about the small space.

I stare dully at his large hands, eyeing the bit of blood drying beneath one of his now-blunted fingernails—the one I accidentally cut too short mere hours ago. The one that made a dying man drifting in and out of drugged consciousness flinch. My last act of service to him in this life, and I managed to taint it.

I'm not ready for this. There's still so much to do—so many memories to make. I don't want to make them on my own.

More head lulling. More agonizingly slow minutes passing.

By 3:30, my husband orders me to bed, promising to let me know if anything changes. But lying down doesn't help as memories flood behind my closed lids, and I fight against the thought of the new ones I'll make without Dad in the future. *He's going to die.* Right in the room that I took my first steps in. Right under the ceiling fan he had to duck under as he passed through to his bedroom—where us kids stared after him, wide-eyed, the one time he didn't dip low enough. Dad didn't say a word; he just reached up to stop the light's swaying before continuing on. In that little room, where we gathered for Christmas, movies, carving pumpkins, shelling pecans, game nights. . . . In the room he's slept in for over a year because his own bed was too painful to sleep in. In the room now transformed into a make-shift hospital with pill bottles replacing the picture frames and home decor on the shelves.

In the room I will never see the same way again.

How has it come to this? Death is supposed to be some foreign thing, far off in the distance. Not here, not now. But, as much as I hate it—fear it—I know deep down that it's far more merciful for the end to come. To remember the father I had. Full of life. Full of wisdom. The one person I could rely on for anything, even when we butted heads because we were too much alike to back down. Even dying, he's still a shadow of his old self, with a full head of hair that grew back after years of chemotherapy and radiation. But I don't want to remember the crippled form dying a room away—a body now riddled with bedsores and swollen, shiny skin where the blood pools. A body too tired and sick to fight anymore.

My husband's hands gently shake me awake. Aunt Vickie says it's close now. She would know. Cancer's already claimed her husband and a son. Now, her younger brother will follow.

I trail my husband into the living room to join my two siblings, brother-in-law, aunt, uncle, and mother—whose keening sobs I know will haunt me for years to come. My heart twists and tears further when I realize Grandma and Grandpa will not make it here before Dad's gone.

The tears flow freely now as we gather around the couch, all eyes fixed on Dad's barely moving chest. Rise . . . fall . . . rise . . . fall . . . rise. . . .

He stills after a soft, barely audible exhale.

He's gone.

GONE. Just like that, on a tiny puff of air that punctuates his entire existence. So soft. So quiet. An injustice to the man who lived fully and loved deeply but perfect for the man whose last words were "thank you" and "I love you."

I will never hear him laugh again. Never hear him teasingly call me his favorite blonde child again. Never see him in this house again. Never again. Never again. NEVER. Again.

Heaviness settles, soul-crushing and final, like someone has plunged a vicious hand through my heart to rip out its center, left to slowly beat and mend but never completely heal. And yet . . . I feel relief. Numbing, horrible, comforting relief. And guilt chasing on its heels for being grateful it's finally over. No more waiting. No more guessing. No more fearing I won't be there when it happens.

5:00 a.m., the thermostat says: the time Dad would be leaving for work if this were a normal Thursday morning. If he were still here. If he weren't gone.

Time is up.

Time. That thing we think we will never run out of.

Until we do.

I THINK I'M JESUS

LORRAINE JEFFERY

I think I'm Jesus or God

he tells me while his serious,
brown eyes bore into mine,
and I will my eyes not
to leak,
under any circumstances.

He continues. *You know that war at the end
of the world? I've already fought it
and won, but they
won't leave me alone.*

Who won't?

*The spirits and souls that go in and out
of my body. I can see them
but can't stop them, and
they make me tired.*

On the couch opposite me,
I'm not seeing the forty-seven-year-old
man but the twice-abandoned
four-year-old cuddled on my lap,
before car seats, on the drive home
after his third adoption.

At fifteen, he saw things
move and speak that couldn't
move or speak—the brambles
already forming in his brain.

I know what he has ridden the bus
two thousand miles to ask,
and my root-deep hope
drinks hemlock and wilts,
head down to rotting earth.

Do you believe me?
And I hear his child voice—
I'm okay, right?
I'm like everybody else—
while somehow knowing
he isn't.

ABOUT THE AUTHORS

Kylie N. Birch spent her youth playing in haystacks and riding horses in the foothills like any respectable child from a farm town would. Her love of sports lead her to the field of education as a health and P.E. teacher for at-risk youth. Kylie now spends her time as a wife and ringleader to three cats and three adorable, extremely energetic children ages five and under. Between nap times and preschool, Kylie has discovered her passion for writing and is excited to navigate her way in a world where a little imagination makes a blank page come to life.

Tracey Gendron Boyle lives about fifty miles from New Orleans, Louisiana. After retiring from a career in state budget, she is doing something she has always wanted to do; return to school to obtain a master's degree in creative writing. She hopes to never stop learning. Tracey loves to read and write, and enjoys long walks in her neighborhood.

Liz Christensen is the host and producer of the "In the Telling" podcast. She is a writer, director, choreographer, film actress, audiobook narrator, and hiker. The youngest of 13 children in a blended family, she is the mother of two teenagers and married to the love of her life. Her best scars come from being an obstacle course racer. She graduated magna cum laude from the University of Utah with a BFA and is pursuing her Masters of Arts in English Teaching. You can find more of her work at lizzylizzyliz.com.

Kevin Lane Dearinger is a retired Broadway performer and English teacher. His poetry has appeared in a wide range of publications. Other works include three theatre histories and two memoirs, *Bad Sex in Kentucky* (2019) and *Onstage with Bette Davis* (Spring 2022). Plays: *Regarding Mrs. Carter* and *Naked on Request.*

Denis Feehan is the past president of Heritage Writers Guild in St George, Utah. As an author, Denis has published 13 poems and 3 short stories. He is the keyboard player in the classic rock band - Time Machine. Denis has been an actor and director in theaters in Los Angeles and Mesquite, NV.

A retired surgeon, **Greg Goodman** is a life-long learner. He is fortunate to be sharing that experience with Kathy who has always helped him to find life's poetry in the real world.

Amy Lynn Hardy, originally of Buffalo, NY, is a 36-year-old budding author of poetry, short stories and a novel. Publications include "Durmitor" (Showbear Family Circus), "Love in a Time of Corona" (Poet's Choice), "Doubt" (zines + things) and "Once Upon a Future Goals List" (UB Honors Magazine). When she isn't writing, she is teaching English and

French at a German High School in Bremerhaven, Germany, giving Zumba Fitness classes and spending time with her cat, Mister Sessels.

Aren K. Hatch has been writing genre fiction since they were seven years old. Their passion for words, languages, and space has been with them for as long as they can remember and has only grown with time. While they love to write about a myriad of topics, they primarily focus on the same core ideas: found families, people of all different backgrounds coming together, a love of languages, and finding and holding on to hope when everything seems bleak. Currently, they are a member of the League of Utah Writers, living in Salt Lake City with their two cats.

Lorraine Jeffery has a bachelor's degree in English, a MLIS in library science, and has managed public libraries in Texas, Ohio and Utah. She has won poetry prizes in state and national contests and published over one hundred poems in journals and anthologies, including *Clockhouse, Kindred, Calliope, Ibbetson Street, Rockhurst Review, Orchard Street Press, Bacopa Press*, League of Utah Writers, *Two Hawks, Riverfeet, Regal Publishing* and *Naugatuck River Review*. Her short stories and essays have appeared in many publications, including *Persimmon Tree, Focus on the Family, Mature Years, Elsewhere* and League of Utah Writers Anthologies. She lives in Utah with her husband.

McKel Jensen is an award-winning writer whose work has appeared in numerous anthologies and online publications. Like many, she is inspired by the world around her and tries to make sense of it through writing. Words create a curious path when they are linked together. McKel holds an MA in English

Literature from Weber State University, a BA in Literary Studies from Utah State University and has worked as a technical writer for several years. McKel is currently a busy mom of three young kids and resides in Brigham City, Utah with her husband.

Grace Diane Jessen lives with her husband Gordon in Glenwood, Utah, where they raised their seven daughters. She is a lifetime member of the League of Utah Writers and a member of the Utah State Poetry Society. Many of her poems have been published and found success in contests. She appreciates the League of Utah Writers and the many ways it has blessed her life.

Rachelle Knapp stays up too late. She writes poetry about things that distract her during the day. She lives in San Diego and part-time in Salt Lake City. You may find her on the beach slipping rocks in her pocket or walking through the snow carrying stacks of children's books from the library to read to tiny ears who will listen. Rachelle is the recipient of the Olive Woolley Burt Award for light verse. You may read more of her poetry in the *Acorn Review*.

C. H. Lindsay is an award-winning poet & writer, housewife, and book-lover. She currently has short stories and poems in sixteen anthologies, with two more coming out next year. Her poems have appeared in several magazines, including *The Leading Edge: A Magazine of Science Fiction and Fantasy*, *Amazing Stories*, and *Space and Time Magazine*. She is working on three novels, five short stories, and two dozen poems (more or less). In 2018 she became Al Carlisle's literary executor. She now publishes his true crime, as well as Floyd C. Forsberg's, under Carlisle Legacy Books, LLC, with plans to add more books in the coming years. She is a member of SFWA, HWA, SFPA, and LUW. She is a founding member of the Utah Chapter of the Horror Writers Association. Mostly blind, she lives in Utah with her "seeing-eye husband," youngest child, and a cat.

September Roberts published her fourth book, *Love on Location*, with The Wild Rose Press in 2018. She writes romance that's smoking hot and always happy ever after.

Joyce Schmid's recent work appears or is forthcoming in *Five Points, Literary Imagination, Dunes Review, New Ohio Review*, and other journals and anthologies. She lives in Palo Alto, California, with her husband of over half a century.

Rufo Tolentino writes screenplays, short stories, and editorials. Obsessed with film and the original Twilight Zone series, his writing has elements of science fiction and psychological thriller. Rufo is an active member of the Salt City Genres Writers chapter of the League of Utah writers. He married his wife Rebecca in July 2021 and is a new homeowner in the Taylorsville area.

Marie Tollstrup taught for thirty-nine years. At Jordan High School in North Long Beach, she founded and advised *Stylus*, a national award-winning literary/arts magazine for twenty-three years. In retirement, Marie focuses on poetry, but branches out to articles, short stories, and creative non-fiction which she enters into local, state, and national contests, winning awards for speaking her mind and poetic word play. Read some of her published poems and prose in League of Utah Writers publications.

Heidi Voss has been practicing making non-dairy yogurt all pandemic and still can't consistently get a good batch. To send her tips on how to make yogurt correctly, you can contact her on her website, authorheidivoss.com. While you're there, you can also download a free short story but that won't help her with her yogurt problem.

Johnny Worthen is an award-winning, multi-genre, tie-dye-wearing author, voyager, and damn fine human being! Trained in literary criticism and cultural studies he earned his Bachelors and Masters degrees from the University of Utah. Beyond English, on a good day, he speaks Danish and reads Latin. He is a Utah Writer of the Year. An avowed Deconstructionist, Johnny writes up-market stories from the inside out, beginning with theme and pursuing an idea through whatever genre will best serve it. So far, he has brought out novels in mystery, young adult, comedy, urban fantasy, horror, and science fiction, both indie and traditionally published. A frequent presenter and panelist at writing conferences and fan conventions, he is active in local communities of artists and writers. A long-time volunteer for the League of Utah Writers, the state's oldest and largest writing organization, including President from 2018-2020. When not writing his own stuff, Johnny edits professionally for a small dark fiction press in Los Angeles and teaches Creative Writing at the University of Utah as an Associate Instructor. He lives in Sandy Utah with his wife, sons and cats. There's also a lawn.

Bryan Young works across many different media. His work as a writer and producer has been called "filmmaking gold" by The New York Times. He's also published comic books with Slave Labor Graphics and Image Comics. He's been a regular contributor for the *Huffington Post, StarWars.com, Star Wars Insider magazine, SYFY, /Film,* and was the founder and editor in chief of the geek news and review site *Big Shiny Robot*! He co-authored *Robotech: The Macross Saga* RPG in 2019 and in 2020 he wrote a novel in the BattleTech Universe called *Honor's Gauntlet* which was honored as the best book by a Utah Writer in 2020. He currently serves as the President of the League of Utah Writers. Follow him on Twitter @swankmotron.

MORE FROM THE LEAGUE OF UTAH WRITERS

FIND ALL OF OUR ANTHOLOGIES AT
LEAGUEOFUTAHWRITERS.COM

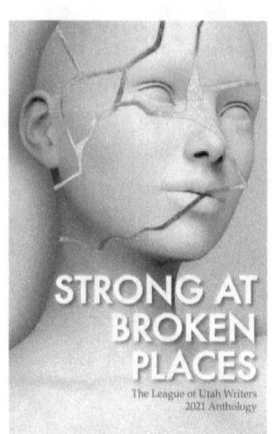

STRONG AT
BROKEN
PLACES

The League of Utah Writers
2021 Anthology

WHAT CAN THE LEAGUE OF UTAH WRITERS DO FOR YOU?

The League of Utah Writers is a non-profit organization dedicated to offering friendship, education, and encouragement to the writers and poets of Utah. Our organization aids our members in the improvement of their craft and support of their goals.

The League of Utah Writers is a vibrant writing community with chapters throughout the state, as well as online with members across the country. Membership in the League of Utah Writers provides support and opportunities for writers and editors at all levels of their careers.

Join us at www.leagueofutahwriters.com

The
Pre-Quill
Conference

Pre-Quill is the League of Utah Writers' Spring writing conference - a day long event of classes, workshops, and networking with other wordsmiths.

This event showcases our local Utah writers in classes and courses geared to each unique voice and talent. It is also a great place to start working on stories, poetry, or any of the other categories listed in the Wooley awards - the League's prestigious contest awarded at the annual Quills conference each year.

Pre-Quill helps refresh your creative neurons with the pulse and energy only spring could bring.

Find more about The Pre-Quill Conference at
www.leagueofutahwriters.com

THE
QUILLS
CONFERENCE

The League of Utah Writers invites you to join us for the Quills Conference, hosted locally in Salt Lake City annually near the end of summer.

The Quills Conference is the League's premium event, bringing in special guest authors, agents, editors, and publishers from around the nation.

This four-day writing conference is for everyone from the fresh voices not yet published to the well-established writers seeking to make a difference in their writing community.

The Quills Conference's annual banquet is also home to The Woolley Awards writing contest and the Quill Awards for published works.

Find out more about Quills at
www.leagueofutahwriters.com

www.ingramcontent.com/pod-product-compliance
Lightning Source LLC
Chambersburg PA
CBHW022155260626
47155CB00018B/1977